Life's Tangled Trail
Revolutionary Fiction
Nathan J Bullock

Preface

Believing the consciousness of most
life to be only in their narrow but tangled
trail of experience, this book has
been written with the idea of helping
the reader's general conception of their
living conditions.
All the characters in this story are
entirely fictitious. And no reference is
intended to any actual person or institution.

Dedicated to:
The advancing parts of civilization.
Both to the leaders on it's changing stage
with life, and the multitude of it's emotional
players with their lives to live

Life's Tangled Trail

Life with it's burdens saved by force;
in spite of our blunders, held it's course.
Then comes confusion as senses react.
We strive to learn whether mystic or fact.
Eventually consciousness, shocking and bold
to solve life's problems, the new and the old.

Editor's Notes

Nathan John Bullock, my grandfather, wrote this novel in the early 1930's. I made an effort to preserve his language and style so that his descendants and others can get to know him and get a taste of what life was like from his viewpoint from 1895 the year he was born to the mid 1930's when he wrote the original manuscript for this work.

I hope that in editing his work my own additions do not take away from his story but instead clarify, give flow to his work, preserve the insights and lessons that were common knowledge to him but may not be to those that haven't experienced the outdoors the way he did. An example is Allen looking at the sun to tell the time of day. To most in our day it may not make sense but to the author that is the best clock when out-of-doors.

Grandfather had great adoration for paleontologists and the scholars of time and believed in the theory of evolution as he tried to expound it on some of these pages. But later as he tried to share his own discoveries with some of these men he thought he admired he was ridiculed, belittled and made fun of by these same great men.

I gathered from this that the thousands of generations that were mentioned in this book may have been reduced to a much shorter period of time in his mind latter on in his life due to other discoveries he made after writing this novel. Perhaps a few thousand years more in line with the Bible.

I loved to listen to his stories much like Allen loved to listen to the stories told by Mr. Harris in this book. He told them in such a way that allowed me to come to my own conclusion of these matters so I will present this story in his words so you can come to your own conclusion about his thought processes in relation to the trying times he experienced.

So let's follow the fictional story of Allen and Helen as they searched for a better way of life for themselves and the people that are sharing the tragedies of the Great Depression.

Marvin C Crowther

Contents

Chapter I

Misfortune

The train whistled while two carefree figures met a short distance from the Rail-road crossing.

"Hello, Helen, What are you doing way out here?"

"How is your father progressing with the oil well?"

"Just fine Allen, how are you. Where have you been keeping yourself lately?"

The train whistled again, it rang in their ears cutting short his answer.

With unexpected suddenness a rending crash drowned out all other sound and violently shook the ground beneath their feet.

Helen Screamed, "Oh, Allen! The train has left the track---Let's go and see if we can help."

They began to run, but their legs felt like they were having to be dragged along in slow motion in their effort to get to the train wreak. The dust and smoke ahead of them seemed a goal to be reached only by desperate and tireless effort.

The roar of escaping steam combined with the shouts of those just arriving and the screams of injured and trapped people made the whole scene one of complete confusion.

Once there, Helen sped to the aid of a young women lying on the ground with a baby folded tightly in her arms, while Allen moved to the assistance of a middle aged man that was helplessly wedged under a table and debris that moments before was part of the dinning car.

With force of effort Allen moved the twisted metal enough to free him from the debris, then lifted and pulled him though a nearby window to a safe place where he could rest comfortably away from the confusion while the rescue attempt that was in process. There were still many passengers trapped in the broken, twisted heaps of wood and metal left by the sudden derailment of the passenger train.

Once settled Allen turned his attention to Helen, to see how she was doing in her efforts to help the women with the baby. He saw Helen sitting next to the cold, lifeless form of the mother, the baby cradled lovingly in her arms. Her lovely eyes gazing into the distance as if envisioning the love, hope and ambition that the unfortunate mother must have had for this little child.

At that moment Allen was distracted by a desperate call for help. He turned toward the train to listen so he could discover the direction of the call. To his relief it was repeated, thou weaker but loud enough that he was able to detect that the sound was coming from the other end of the dining car. He ran to a window, looked through and saw no one inside.

Instead he heard heavy breathing coming from a pile of tables, chairs, table-covers, dishes and fixtures that were once the spender of the modern dining car. He climbed through the window and looked around the tangled mass until he found the disheveled form of a respectably dressed gray-haired elderly man with a cut just over the right eye.

Quickly Allen removed the debris that trapped the elderly man. His weak cry for help was attempted again but now only amounted to a slight whisper. The man lapsed into unconsciousness by the time Allen worked his way through the debris to reach him. Then with great effort he carried the limp form to the window then with care because of the badly injured chest and legs lifted him through the window and settled him on the ground near Helen and the newly orphaned baby. Once he loosened the vest, tie and belt to help him breath more freely, he looked over at Helen who was still sobbing. The impact of the whole situation brought a tremor to his voice as he spoke, "Helen you must get control of yourself. . . the baby needs your attention... please if the old gentleman comes to; take care of him, I will be back in a moment."

Allen spoke over his shoulder as he ran to the front of the train where the conductor was overseeing the care of the engineer and a couple other passengers. He wanted to find out if help had been called yet. The conductor assured him that the railroad authorities were working with the local police and fire departments. Aid was on its way.

Confident that help would soon be there he returned to check on the elderly man who, was now becoming conscious, his eyelids flickered as his eyes slowly opened, it looked like he was becoming partially aware of the situation and should be alright.

Helen stopped sobbing when she heard the sounds of sirens. She stood up while still holding the baby to see if there was something she could do to help Allen aid the injured.

A truck attended by a patrolman on a motorcycle came close to them and stopped. A man, that appeared to be a doctor, got out of the truck and joined the patrolman as they walked over to the women whose baby Helen was holding in her arms. The doctor lifted her hand, felt for the pulse but the feel of the cool flesh was answer enough. He then nodded to the patrolman then started toward the first man Allen had taken from the wreck to evaluate his condition.

Meanwhile the patrolman began to look for something to identify the woman, finding none he turned her on her side to see if anything may have fallen beneath the body. He was unsuccessful so he held the baby for Helen so she could aid in a closer search. She discovered a letter in the bosom of the dress.

The patrolman looked over the letter for a moment then walked over and interrupted the doctor who was just finishing with his patient and said, "Say, Doc, this letter is from a hardhearted old boy, even in this cruel old world of ours, listen to this:

Mrs. J.T. Craige:

Upon receipt of your letter appealing for financial aid, I wish to call your attention to the fact: that John was disinherited on the date of your wedding, which as you know, was against my wishes. Please except this as final.

With Respect

B.A. Craige

"Yes, Bill, that letter is very cruel, but we find plenty of that these days. Give me a hand with bandaging this fellow."

The doctor was helping the elderly gentleman but was having trouble holding him while bandaging the cut over his eye.

At that time Allen was searching for water in the coach ahead because he saw a man coming out of it with water in his hat. He already saw that the dining car was too badly crushed to still have any water left in it.

Allen converted his own hat to hold water when he arrived there. When he returned he was able to offer the elderly man a drink who relished the water then showed his appreciation with a smile.

He pointed to the letter that the patrolman was sharing with the doctor and related a brief history of the people mentioned in it, "He was a college professor of economics, B.A. Craige and I were born and reared in the same town. The lady." He motioned to the still form of the young women, "Craige's daughter-in-law and I met on the train where she told me the story of her past. She told how just a few months after her baby was born her husband had been killed, leaving her to face the world without the means to keep herself and the baby. When we met she was changing location so they could start over."

The doctor at that point began to hurry the patients aboard the truck so he could get them to the hospital. The professor noticed the fat dimpled face of the baby peeking out of the covers he was wrapped in and asked, "May I take the baby to the hospital with me?"

Helen reluctantly consented, in just this short time she had become so attached and concerned for the infant that the idea of parting brought tears to her eyes.

Allen helped the police officer finish loading the baby's mother and the middle aged man into the truck, this accomplished, they directed their efforts to lift the professor carefully into the truck so they wouldn't aggravate his injuries.

Once he was settled comfortably in the truck Helen handed the baby to Allen then stood back and watched as he placed the cooing bundle carefully on the professor's lap.

Goodbyes were said all around and the young pair promise to come visit the professor at the hospital as the driver forced the motor to gather momentum and jerkily steered the truck over the littered uneven road.

Once the truck disappeared from sight Allen's attention was drawn to a smartly attired young man that was looking in and around the crumpled cars. He pointed him out to Helen, " I wonder who that is that is in such a hurry, he seems to be looking for something."

Bill the police officer replied," That's Tony, the newspaper hound. He just started as a reporter recently. He used to run the newsstand down at Joe's place."

Tony Recognized his friend Bill and started toward them, "Hello Bill, you got any news for me?"

"Sure, just sent two males badly bruised, a baby and one dead women with some history to county."

Upon hearing this Tony looked up from his notebook with interest, reached into his pocket, produced a five dollar bill and tucked it into Bill's hand. Then returned his attention to his notebook and prepared once more to write.

Allen looked at Helen and stated; "Helen, you look all tired out, come, let's go home."

"Yes, Allen, I did little but now the excitement has died down I feel shaky, and a little bewildered by all that has happened."

"So long fellows, we'll see you later." they said as they left Bill and Tony.

Helen needed support so Allen put his arm around her waist to help her slowly move away from the wreck. He guided her steps along the narrow trail then through a field where the rustle of the ankle deep alfalfa was soothing to her strained nerves.

Helen's weight shifted slightly, Allen wondered how her usually cheery mother would react to the train wreck interfering with the family routine. The many years she had been married to Helen's father, she had been left at home with the children to fret over his safety and health, while her husband, a geologist, traveled to various dangerous parts of the world to participate in important projects.

Allen always liked to be around the friendly father who continually had friends and acquaintances came to him for help and advice on geology, business and personal problems. He remembered the time his own mother had gone over to get advice from Mr. Harris on settling her parents estate. He was able to help her understand the legal talk and simplify the process for her. He also remembered when he was quite young he and his mother were visiting the Harris' when she opened a letter she had received earlier that day. When she read it she swooned and fell on the floor. Mr. Harris gently awakened her, then when she regained consciousness tears welled up in her eyes and she sobbed. She gathered up the letter and clasped him tightly in her arms. Her despair seemed complete as he tried to console and help her the short distance between our two homes.

Allen could never forget the words Mr. Allen used to try to calm her; "The war department often makes mistakes in recording the casualty lists."

His thoughts then went to the last visit at her home, Helen's mother directed him to the study where Mr. Harris was just completing a report on the "Historical Geology of the Earth and Biological Evolution of Man."

Allen was distracted by the fascinating rocks, fossils, and pictures that were arranged around the study. It was these marvelous curiosities that were his play things in the past that had since become objects of interest now. How focused and intense his attention became the many times Mr. Harris explained the history of a fossil, such as a bit of fossilized seaweed.

He said this type of seaweed had laid deep in the earth for millions of years until an upheaval brought it closer to the surface where it was discovered. A long time ago in the history of time this seaweed grew in abundance in the shallow parts of the ocean.

Around and among it crawled flat dish-like creatures who, were the owners of the oceans domain. As they developed and multiplied into large numbers the conditions around them changed. Other creatures of importance developed. One of these had a body that was longer in shape, its legs extended further from the body. This one had an interest in life that caused his eyes to extend from his body a short way. The ambition of this creature to feel everything he came near caused it to developed a pair of large hands (claws) t hat had a vise-like grip.

Along with this lobster like creature developed many kinds of tiny bug-like creatures. These creatures became so numerous in the most fertile part of the ocean that they became a menace to the lobster. So the lobster moved deeper or crawl under bits of dead seaweed to wait for these little creatures to pass. He would move but little while they were close then only if the seaweed covered him so he would not be noticed.

Over time the the slime on his body came in contact with the lime that was abundant on the ocean floor and eventually hardened and provided a protective exterior skeleton. This exoskeleton provided the protection he needed to be able to move more freely from place to place on the ocean floor.

New creature's that had the ability to protect themselves and migrate around the ocean brought about noticeable changes in the plant life in this vast expanse of ocean. The plants became more abundant as they feed the ever multiplying creatures. Each form of life was adjusting and moving to the places that provided the most abundant supply of food with the least danger in procuring it.

Mounds began to slowing but surely rise from the floor of the ocean to develop into hills and long ridges of corral. These were the result of numerous small animals gathering and building rock material around themselves to protect themselves from the trampling hordes of other creatures and to keep from being submerged in the deepening ooze at the ocean floor. Within these hills and ridges resided the tiny lobster like creature that sat at the entrance of his tunnel grasping tiny plants that floated by. Each day as he ate and took care of business he would add a little to his tunnel until he had room for a mate and new generations of his kind.

When the lobster like creature died, the young would close him off in the tunnel in the process of expanding their home into ever larger ridges of coral. In this process both the creatures that lived in the ocean and those that died combined together to build the coral up until it reached the surface of the water. The work of these little creatures continually changed the shape of the ocean floor.

A new shadow disturbed the entire scene as a new species that developed. This new creature squirmed with a peculiar motion that taxed its poor strength and skin as it twisting from side to side. The ability to swim, though awkwardly, gave it more freedom than the crawling creatures. The ability to travel allowed it to come in contact with other creatures, some that were larger and swifter. Some of these were fearsome looking with gills that enabled them to take more oxygen from the water so they had more vigor and strength enabling then to pursue and eat the slower and less vigorous inhabitants of the abundant ocean. In time the best protected or swiftest survived and the unprotected or clumsy perished.

Into this panorama of these memories of the professor's stories of the prehistoric past came the reflection of a rounded pink cheek and a well-formed nose above which were eyes of a deep ocean blue, these were looking intently into his. Unconsciously they had wandered off the path and had taken the long way home. With a grin reflecting the pleasure that was showing on each of their faces that had spread into cheery smiles, her question came to him as a shock.

"Allen, why are you so quiet?"

"I'll try not to be from now on, I was thinking of the past when we were smaller. Do you remember when your father would take us into his library and show us the pictures of those rocks and fossils that were on the walls about the room?

I often think of them and wonder what relation they have to our present surroundings."

Yes, Allen, but your reflections are not edible and I'm hungry. Come let's run a ways."

There was a flutter of shirts and a click of shoes as she run along the path with Allen taking the cue and racing along with her.

They soon came up on an old couple, both were waving their arms and threatening each another. As the young couple slowed down to get their breath they couldn't help but listen as they shouted their words of misunderstanding at each other.

"I won't have the young scalawag around. He ain't no good anyway." The old gentleman exclaimed as he brought his fist down with a spat on the other hand.

"Yes, but, John remember she's our daughter and you used to think he was alright." she hissed as she shook her finger threateningly under his nose.

"Mary, you know, he just keeps harping about sharing the wealth." He shot back as he deliberately took aim at a rock as if to prove he had not chewed tobacco these many years without a fair degree of marksmanship.

"Yes, Pa, but you don't see his meaning about wealth." She defended.

Then with a flash of fire in his eyes he replied, "He ain't got none."

Helen, now rested from their invigorating run that had brought them within earshot of so strange an argument, tugged at Allen's arm and reminded, "I hate to miss the end of this, I'd really like to learn how the son-in-law fares, but we are home."

"Favoring Allen with a hopeful smile she added. "I'd like to have you come in and help me explain to mother the reason for my being tardy."

"Sorry, Helen, but my mother expected me home awhile ago. I should get home and clean up before company arrives. Tell your mother I will see her when I call for you, remember, we promised to visit our new found friends at the hospital tomorrow."

"See you tomorrow." She said as she skipped along the path leading to the house. Her cheery words reflected her vigor, vitality and her youthful beauty.

Chapter II

Home's Appeal

His thoughts once again went to the professor as he hurried along the path to Helen's home. There was an air of importance about him that demanded respect. Not so much the demand for the respect that dignity and authority demand, but one of friendliness, that invites one to talk and confide. His wondering thoughts distracted him from seeing the bent figure in the garden at first. Helen was busily picking delicate flowers that appeared to have the color painted on, with petals that reminded him of the multi-colored butterflies that are so abundant here in the summer and fall.

He glanced up with an expression of pleasure when she called his name with that delicate touch which is such a feminine attraction. As he was aroused from his wandering thoughts she artfully put her hair in place and revealed a smile of pleasant satisfaction that seemed to say, 'what a pleasure to see you.'

"I suppose you would have passed me right up had I not called to you? Come and help me finish this bouquet for mother and I'll be ready to go."

Nonplussed for a moment he then explained, "You sure caught me napping that time. Pick flowers?

Say that reminds me of our walks along the creek when we were little."

When they were done they presented the flowers to Mrs. Harris, these greatly cheered her, in turn she rewarded them with her wonderful smile and waved to them as they briskly walked down the path on their way to the hospital.

Their fast pace soon brought them to the hospital entrance, once there they walked more slowly to allow themselves time to study their surroundings. That feeling came to them that told them they were trespassing on sacred ground that had been set apart by some powerful, ancient god who was watching over it. They were almost expecting that ancient God himself to meet them at every step.

Once passed the front door, the inside of the building appeared to be an orderly well-organized machine. Where the characters involved were expected to give their utmost effort, strength and moral. Each attendant cheerfully preformed their duties as though the narrow walls about them bounded the entire world and their lives were narrowed to the work at hand. One of the attendants noticing that they seemed confused by the unfamiliar place approached them, "Who do you want to see?"

They indicated, "Professor Hopkins" and were quickly escorted to his room.

They found the professor lying in a bed of white, with a happy smile on his face. He was expecting them because he heard their footsteps before the door slowly opened. Once the door opened they timidly looked into the room and approached his bed.

"Your appearance at this time proves my faith in the youth of today. I felt sure you would come." With this said the professor turned upon his side. Immediately an attendant hurried over to him who the professor instructed to raise the bed to a slightly elevated position, that made him more comfortable while he was talking.

He thanked the attendant, turned to the pair and said, "Allen, if you will look in the drawer of that stand you will find a box of candy, I hope you young folks will accept it as a small token of my appreciation of your visit with me today."

Allen noticed the professor's eagerness to see if it pleased them, so he tried to put off the feeling of timidity as he procured the box of candy and handed it to Helen as he replied, "Mr. Hopkins, both Helen and I have been in a state of excitement and anticipation since we left home, hoping that we might find you well enough to come and visit a few days at our home. I know mother will be pleased if you will accept."

Helen saw the professor's eyes close slightly as a look of longing came into them.

There was a moment of silence that was broken at last by Helen. "Do come. The folks will surely be disappointed if you don't. When father learned of your identity he was very interested. He is a geologist, and would like to exchange ideas with you."

At this the professor immediately became interested for this life was most dear to him. The one pleasure he cherished above all others was to meet someone with whom he could exchange views on the world's problems.

He then nodded his head saying. "you young folks surely bring me happiness to find you so interested in me at such a moment of my life, and of course your father's credentials add a special inducement, I accept the invitation and hope I may help to make my visit as interesting to you as it will surely be to me."

At this moment they were interrupted by the musical voice of a nurse proclaiming; "Visiting hours are over."

Both pleasantly bid the professor goodbye, then started homeward.

Upon returning to the Harris's home they came into the middle of a discussion, as they stepped in they heard Helen's mother reply, "But, Herbert, I believe Royal is better adapted as your assistant for he has two years of preparation in geology."

With a sympathetic understanding for his wife's reply, Helen's father returned. "Yes, dear, but Royal's religious attitude retards him from having a correct understanding of geology and it's proper application."

Mrs. Harris had seen the outcome of her husband's judgment in what seemed more important happenings many times before. She was not a stubborn type, rather one to appreciate the importance of such judgment so she conceded, "After all, dear, he is to be your assistant not mine."

Helen's mother was just putting the final touch on the food she was arranging on the table as Allen and Helen came in, flushed by the excitement of their recent trip to the hospital.

Helen could hardly wait until she related to her father the professor's acceptance, so with a sudden outburst exclaimed, "Father he is going to come."

Happily she ran forward and threw her arms around his neck, the one thing she liked to do it was to please him.

Mrs. Harris, being practiced in handling awkward situations, reminded, "Helen, please take Allen's hat, dinner is waiting."

With the ordinary formalities, happy remembrances and a joke or two the meal was soon over. Then with a slight touch on the arm Mr. Harris led Allen toward the study.

To Allen the arrangement of the study was about as usual, except there were pictures, books and many other things that he had not seen there before.

Mr. Harris did not give him time to investigate for he preceded immediately with the subject that was on his mind. "My, boy, you have grown to near manhood in the small narrow limits of this city, you have been a comfort to your mother and a morale inspiration to those around you, but there is one thing you have not done."

He then sat back in his chair and waited a moment to watch the affect of his remarks,

"The occasion has never arisen to make you conscious of it, but in the near future you are going to have to prepare the way for yourself."

Mr. Harris settled back in his chair again, giving the youth time to consider. Now Allen had become so overwhelmed by anticipation of what was about to be said that he was unable to speak.

Helen's father sensing this began, "It is not my purpose to belittle or embarrass you, but I want to offer you an opportunity to help me. I have become weary of continuous travel and business responsibility, therefore, I've made arrangements in my business to use an assistant. Allen, I believe you have the proper interest and ability.

Now, with the actual experience and the responsibilities you will have, you can develop yourself materially, thus shifting the load of financial worry from the shoulders of your mother to your own. Now, I do not wish to receive an answer at the present time, but think it over, discuss it with your mother, then give me your answer later.
Come now, Helen and her mother are waiting for us."

When they returned to the dinning room the women had already cleared the dishes, put away the leftovers and were having a short discussion as to what would be best for the evening's entertainment. Mrs. Harris suggested singing. This left the lead to Helen, so with the ease of one having the ability to keep such a situation in hand she placed herself at the piano and proceeded to play and old southern folk song.

Soft strains of music calmed Allen's nerves that were made tense thinking about entering a new world that he had not previously been part of.

Helen's mother interrupted his thoughts when she broke the silence, "Shall we all sing the chorus?"

Allen shifted his attention to the musical strains of the old folk song but as those around him began to sing, he joined in and was soon carried into the pleasure of the evening.

In time Mr. and Mrs. Harris begged to be excused from the evenings entertainment to prepare for important business that they needed to attend to at an early hour the next day.

The soft vibrating music of the piano carried Allen's feelings along with it was joined by the appealing voice of Helen singing a love song. It told of loneliness for a lover and a beating heart that wished to be consoled, this carried him on to accept the appeal and he became a willing victim whose being cried for consolation and friendship.

The song soon finished and as Helen arose their eyes met. The quickening throb of their hearts and the fleeting moments of silence began to make of their blushes an awkward situation.

Helen freed herself from the tenseness of the moment and remarked, "Would you care to look at the pictures of my friends and relatives?"

This he accepted with the hope that he might regain his composure. As the pictures were turned the reminders on the back told much of the history of the south. Her mother's folks were southern people for many generations, and they reminded Helen of the many stories that had been told her of the South in the days of slavery, the Civil War and the loss of many relatives. There was the picture of one who had been a chaplain and had been much revered by the family.

Finally they came to the pictures of girls many of whom Allen knew form school. There were also pictures of many boys, these each received special comments for they had all been Allen's chums.

Helen chose one and handed it to him with a light comment, "You remember Royal, do you not?

He has been away most of the time the last two years. He comes to talk to father about geology and usually spends an hour or two with mother and I, telling of his experiences at college."

Allen thought he detected too much pleasure in her expression as she called his attention to the picture she passed to him.

He noticed there was a little more color in her cheeks then before. This made his thoughts go racing back to his first memory of Royal. They had been in the same class together up to the eighth grade. There had been nothing to mar their friendship, only the usual games of swimming and joking together until Royal's father had received an inheritance. After that Royal was sent to private schools and finally to college. He had not seen him after that, but had heard of him attending social events that involved only those who were recognized as well-to-do.

Having this in mind, he replied, "Yes, Helen, we were chums at school together. Surly you remember that, Will you please sing again?"

With a smile of wonderment she arose and in that short distance to the piano she experienced a thrill, one that had made her appreciate the nearness of one so able to control his emotions and still return her warmth of friendliness. For Allen smilingly put his arm around her waist and together they sang the songs of adventure and love that best fit their mood.

Time passed as it always does, Allen took a quick glance at the clock, that has been relentlessly ticking it's way along hour after hour, and was surprised at how late it was, he knew he should be going.

He assisted Helen to her feet and took both her hands in his. "Helen, this has been the most enjoyable moment of my life, seeing you in the light of womanhood, for we have been but children at play in the past."

Allen was carried by the events of the day to an exhalation, in which, he he took a look at past, saw mistakes and decided not to repeat them.

Helen saw the change in him, but was unable to understand the cause but with a determination to find out she blushingly replied, "You too have changed, everything seems different now." Her voice was slightly uncontrolled. "You know we are no longer children."

The truth of her feelings became clear and she smiled to conceal her confusion as their desire of the moment was met, Allen embraced her in his first good night kiss.

Next morning as Allen awoke it was with the remembrance of his evening with Helen. Gradually upon this picture of her in his embrace crept the truth of what Helen's father had told him. He played while spending the money his mother had given him without a thought of how it might be regained or from whence it had come. This left him feeling as though he had been stealing his mother's pie. Shadowing all this was the realization that he would have to face his mother with a complete confession of his laxness of the past.

In an attempt to free himself from this feeling, he jumped from bed with a determination to meet the world face to face. He hurriedly dressed and was soon in the kitchen.

"Mother, may I help with breakfast?"

This was his first attempt to help her, in surprise his mother answered, "Why, Allen: what is it?--where are you going so early?"

Allen saw she did not understand him and with a flushed face replied, "No, mother, there is something I wanted to talk to you about. But let me help you with breakfast first."

The morning meal was soon prepared and on the table. Allen had taken an interest with only a few displays of awkwardness as he learn the art of preparing a meal.

Allen's mother seemed very worried as she finished her meal. This was not in the ordinary routine of life for her son to take such an interest in her. She had watched over and cared for him since he was an infant. He was the only child and with no other with whom to divide her attention, giving to him had became her life's work, without the expectation of reward or service in return.

Allen took his mother's arm and together they seated themselves on the divan for a heart-to-heart talk.

"Now, mother, I would like to know something of our past, a part of which I have never inquired about. Where did we get our income and of what does it consist?"

Allen's mother, beginning to see he had discovered the truth concerning their slowly diminishing means of support, answered. "Allen, is there something you have needed? What have you heard to cause you to ask these serious questions?"

Her worn body shuddered and her face clouded as though she feared that which might follow.

But Allen knew his mother well enough to not linger in the telling of last nights awakening. With faltering voice he told her the truth that had taken root, how he had been offered the job as assistant, because of Mr. Harris's duties in other fields of work and his ill health.

Allen's mother listened with a worried frown, which deepened into a look of dismay, as tears began to flow down her motherly face. This was a moment in her life which she dreaded would come up some day. The truth she had tried to hide from him, that there would be a time to come when he would have to take responsibility, possibly leave home and a broken hearted mother behind. She had yearned for the love of her dead husband these many years and knew she would someday be separated from her son.

His mother's tears almost stopped him from responding, but he gathered his scattered wits and lovingly tried to console her. "Mother, I don't have to give him my answer right away. Let's consider it for a time for there are more questions I would like to ask Mr. Harris."

He tried to turn the trend of thought into another channel, "Mother, the professor has promised to visit us a day or two before he goes home. He is also going to visit at Helen's for awhile. Don't you think that will be nice? He is such a fatherly old gentleman."

As she listened she thought she saw or heard a tinge of feeling as Allen spoke of Helen. They had been close together the last few days.

Was it possible Allen had awakened to manhood?

She turned her eyes toward him, and immediately saw there had been a change in him since she last scanned his face.

Allen noticed his mother did not answer at once and sensed she was reviewing memories of which he had no recollection, he said: "Helen's father has heard of him many times and is very anxious to meet and talk to him."

At this time there came a knock at the door.

Chapter III

Through Time

The conversation quieted as Allen's mother brushed away most of the lines of worry and tears and stepped away to answer the door, she revealed a smiling face that to Allen was an inspiration. Her smile was one she knew gave men courage to meet the battles of life, but to his mother at this moment it only intensified the dread in her heart of the immediate future.

She tried to control her feelings as she faltered, "Won't you come in Helen?"

Helen felt there was a curious tone to her voice, one she had not noticed in the many years of visits to Allen's home, she replied, "Father sent me over but I don't want to intrude if you are busy."

Allen sensed the coldness that was developing between them as he walked to the door and broke in, "Helen, do come in. Mother and I were just talking about your father's offer to me."

Helen responded to the appeal in his voice, stepped through the door and finished her errand. "Allen Father would like you to come and look over some books and new specimens he found on his last trip."

With this she prepared to go while Allen's mother tried to regain her composure, she was turning over in her mind glimpses of the past when this smiling happy girl had come and gone always leaving a cheery feeling behind her, but now she felt as though a slowly darkening night was engulfing her.

Was it that she had allowed jealousy to engulf her and to be the paramount emotion of her life?

Then gradually came a ray of light as the true meaning began to take shape in her confused and bewildered mind. She had never before realized that sooner or later there would come the time in her son's life when he could no longer be sheltered within the limits of her protecting care. But now she must admit he was no longer her baby and must take his place in the world.

This cleared her mind, and all feelings of jealousy were soon cast off. A smile came back to her face as she asked, "Helen, will you please stay while Allen is gone? He will tell your mother where you are."

She walked over to Helen put her arms around her and continued, "Dear, I made a mistake and I may have hurt your feelings. If you will stay, I would like to talk to you about it."

With this sudden turn of events Helen seemed a little puzzled but soon responded, "I nearly forgot to tell you, the professor is coming tomorrow. He called father and had a short talk with him on the phone, father wanted him to come over to our place first, but the professor insisted that he come here. I believe he has become quite attached to you, Allen."

She noticed in Allen's mothers face, a flush of excitement, for it had been many years since there had been a man staying at her home, the preparation for such a guest would take no little effort and a few new arrangements.

There was no doubt in her mind that he would need some special attention until his condition had improved to a degree of health that would be safe for him to travel home.

Allen's mother turned to Helen and with a questioning look inquired. "Will you stay? I need your help more than ever, you and I have a visitor soon and Allen will be gone."

To this earnest appeal Helen answered, "Surely, I told mother that I might stay for awhile."

Allen,was leaving with hat and coat as Helen reminded, "Father wishes you to hurry, for he must ship some of the material soon."

Allen finished putting on his coat, patted Helen on the arm, kissed his mother and called as he went thru the door, "You two be good while I'm gone." and as an added remark, "I'll see you latter."

Both Helen and Allen's mother watched his quick steps as they finally lengthened into a run, carrying him out of sight behind the neighbors shrubbery.

Their eyes met and with a mutual understanding they proceeded to the kitchen to brew a cup of tea.

In a few moments Allen was knocking at the door of Helen's home.

Mrs Harris greeted him cheerfully. "Come right in. You will find Herbert in his study. But say, young man, how is your mother."

Mrs. Harris chatted as they moved toward the study. She stopped at the door and listened inventively while Allen told her of Helen's willingness to stay to help his mother in the preparation for the professor. With the excuse that she had to hurry and prepare dinner, Mrs. Harris opened the study door and called to her husband, "Herbert, take this young man, and give him a good lesson for me. I believe he has kidnapped your daughter," with a smile she left for the kitchen.

"young man, come right in, that is the very thing I had in mind. I have arranged these specimens so we can use them to refer to as I tell their story."

Allen knew what was expected of him so he arranged himself attentively in his chair in preparation for Mr. Harris's lesson.

This was a long story with many rocks, fossils and pictures to corroborate his ideas, taking most of the afternoon with the exception of enough time to eat. Once lunch was finished they repaired themselves to the study to continue the lesson.

In time Allen's head that was now swimming with new ideas came up with a start, "Mr. Harris, I nearly fell asleep, maybe we had better finish this some other time."

This timely expression conveyed to Helen's father that it was getting late, so he replied, "Well, Allen, that was a long trek thru time wasn't it?

It may be best for us to sleep on that much and try to cover the rest of the history on some other occasion."

They left the study and found that the rest of the family had retired. He bid Mr. Harris Good-night and ran briskly home. Upon arrival he found that his mother had already retired so he hurried to bed and was soon asleep. This was not a sound sleep for his dreams seemed to recount the lesson that he just received from Mr. Harris. He was carried back many millions of years through the history of the earth when great fishes floundered about in the shallower parts of the ocean.

The surface of the earth was changing from great plateaus slowly rising from the water that were struck, broke and crumpled by other plateaus that were shoved rapidly to enormous heights. The air stank from countless millions of plants and sea animals that were trapped on land to die and decay or adapt themselves to the new environment.

Over time many varieties of both plants and animals were able to exist. The damp air furnished sufficient moisture for them to grow and reproduce. These improve from one generation to to the next until low green foliage and animals of many varieties existed over all the lands of the earth.

On occasion a plant grew taller until it towered high above the rest. From these developed giant trees that over thousands of generations developed and multiplied until the earth was covered with forests.

This slow change caused the monstrous fishes of the oceans to have trouble procuring food. Their inability to swim fast in the shallow places made it difficult to capture enough prey to satisfy their hunger.

Their ever increasing appetite caused some to develop a long extended neck that they used to reach the ocean bottom so they could eat what they pleased. Their weight made their fins of little use for swimming so they used them to support their heavy bodies while they eased along the shallow, ocean floor. In time the fins developed into thick heavy legs that helped these huge monsters move about on the bottom of the sea.

Over many generations some of them developed lungs that collected oxygen and allowed them to keep their head above the water for longer periods of time. In time a genus came forward that could lumber about on the sandy beaches. With this new found freedom from the water they were able to develop eyesight that helped them see the foliage beyond the beaches, but before they could reach it they had to struggle back to the ocean.

Each new generation developed more ability to travel on land until at last there were creatures that could stay entirely on land where they would lay their eggs and hatch their young. These new varieties developed breathing organs that made it impossible for them to return to the life in the water again. While others developed into numerous herds that used up the plants by the ocean so they were now forced to migrate inland. There they ate the foliage of the trees and raised their young.

Deep bogs of moss and lichen were found in these forests that would mire and hold the tremendous bodies of many of these great beasts that were fossilized to become a record of their existence. Some wiggled out and were able to travel on to more solid ground where they would romp, play and fight.

They would level the vegetation into smooth arenas where they could live for short time until the food was used up so they had to move on. This process was repeated by the great herds until all of the land was filled with animals.

Some of the young proved to be misfits that could not follow the migration so they were left behind to adapt themselves to the conditions around them. Some lived in the swamps or bogs, others in the trees and still others were able to soar short distances in the air. These in their efforts to live made a wriggling, running, climbing and flying mass of life that needed to eat each other to live thereby creating a violent world.

Great beasts moved thru the swamps causing all other life to swim, fly or scamper from their path, for these violent creatures replaced their fines with legs that allowed them to moved in great winding curves, crushing or eating all life they found in their way. These giant monsters learned to either move more swiftly to catch their prey or fight with other monsters to take what they had wrapping around one another, rolling and thrashing about in agonizing grips of death until one of them was killed. Then on to the smaller animals forcing them to learn to hide or leave the swamps to subsist in the forests.

There were other misfits that watched these ponderous herds as they soared overhead. These were ugly dark-colored creatures, who impatiently watched the fighting monsters until their struggles grew slower and slower until they finally ceased. Then with a last final survey of the surrounding conditions they swooped down to the feast.

These ancient buzzards had long gaping jaws that showed two rows of saw-like teeth that were used to tear and eat the flesh of those unfortunate creatures. Many varieties of these flying creatures were searching the earth for the kind of food they most preferred filling the air with large quantities of flying creatures of all sizes who,sprung from the first animals that crept out of the ocean to the earth's surface.

The other creatures fled from these flying creatures to places of safety. Those without legs wiggled into the underbrush of the forest while those with legs ran into the jungle or climbed trees to hide in the branches to watch the tragedies of life as hundreds became meals for these hideous creatures of the air..

One creature found that perching in the treetops was the perfect refuge from the confusion below. Though safe from danger he still needed to find food without exposing himself to the danger above and below. He did this by moving from limb to limb until he found his desired food. Some found a long slim tree that was burdened almost to the breaking point with a great cluster of yellow fruit, the tantalizing odor of which caused moisture to drip from his lips.

He moved close to the tree and ate the well-ripened fruit, that we call a banana.

Once filled with the sweet-smelling fruit, he began to search for water to quench his thirst. He wandered through the branches back to the slanting pathway that he first used to obtain the heights. He returned down to a refreshing pool and took care of his thirst. The old dread of creatures flying above returned so he climbed back to the protection of the trees again. These habits kept his kind living close to the trees for safety.

As a thousand generations of these species lived and died other species of many varieties adapted to live in the trees. One particular kind adapted well to moving from limb to limb and from place to place in the jungle. This one was of great strength and stood on his hind feet which had adapted to be used as hands to help in his swinging from branch to branch. His tail had diminished in size into a slender pliable instrument that aided greatly by holding him to a branch or acting as an extra hand while he gathered fruit or moved through the trees.

This variety grew most abundant and lived on the fruits and nuts of the trees.

Out of this teeming mass of vegetable and animal life of the earth these tree people grew supreme, for they had learned to live in colonies where they grew active and powerful in body but vicious in the protection of themselves and their families and quick to detect the approach of an enemy.

At this very moment slowly and silently a long slim, gray body slipped from the underbrush and advanced to the lower limbs of the trees, wound and twisted to greater heights. A flat-head with cold piercing eyes was followed by the partially coiled slim body trailing down into the jungle foliage and out of sight. The greedy eyes of the hated reptile were always looking into the foliage ahead. He had seen a movement in the upper branches of the trees. He moved slowly winding from limb to limb to get closer to the young of the tree people. Then preparing himself for that last long swing he darted his head forward with lightning-like speed and mercilessly coiled around the intended victim, but not before the baby of the tree people had cried out with a high-pitched scream of terror and pain.

The people of the trees heard this agonized distress call of their young. With terrorizing roars they sprang into action with a cry of rage that was their tribal call to attack. They rushed headlong toward the appeal for help. The mother, sensing the great danger of her baby, was foremost to the rescue with only the baby's screams to guide her. While half blinded in her own rage she spied the figure of one strange among them. The snake lacking arms and legs was almost helpless in comparison to the oncoming angry creature.

The stranger, sensing his own danger, was suddenly gripped with panic. The increasing speed of the oncoming mother disheartened any attempt to flee. His muscles seemed paralyzed and her hot breath burned

his eyes ---- suddenly the spell was broken, his muscles responded
----with every ounce of energy within him----he sprang-----

"Dear me Allen, Don't jump so. I just came to call you for breakfast."

Chapter IV

Family Secrets

"Whew-- Mother, I'm sure glad it was you. Gosh, I guess I ate too much cake before I went to bed. That sure was some nightmare." He rubbed the stiffness from his face and looked around to be sure of his surroundings.

Still frightened, she patted him on the head while reassuring herself there was nothing wrong. "I thought that something has happened to you the way you rolled and tossed about. As I touched you, you jumped up and liked to frightened me to death. About that cake, young man. Helen and I made some dainties yesterday in preparation for Mr. Hopkin's coming. After you broke a piece out of it, instead of using a knife, you set the cake right down on top of them."

By this time Allen realized that his mother was over her fright and was really scolding him. Putting his arm around her, he hugged her tight, kissing her, "Now mother, I didn't mean to. I was so darned tired last night, I hardly remember going to bed. But, I can still taste the flavor of that cake. Gee, I wish I had known those goodies were there, I would have tried them, too."

By this time his mother was smiling, and with a light pinch on his cheek she answered, "That cake was my hard work. But, you will have to answer to Helen for those tarts you mashed. Come, get dressed while I finish preparing breakfast."

She hurried out of the room for she remembered, she had left the toast on the back of the stove and it might burn.

As Allen dressed he began to sum up the results of yesterdays lessons and his thoughtlessness in getting into things last night.

Among the thoughts of all the changes in these creatures over time entered the words of Helen's mother, 'What you learn from Herbert is well and good, but remember the Bible contains a history of the earth. Genesis records that God created the earth and all living thing in six days. Herbert says that the fossils of plants and animals lay in every layer of the earth but I only see them in one or two layers. This supports the history of the flood that washed the earth killing all life that wasn't on the ark, then burying some of the dead to be preserved for you to find as proof of God's word."

His reflections coursed willfully through his head as he dressed and finally they formed into words that were spoke aloud. "Gosh, now I am in a heck of a jam. I spoiled almost all of their afternoon's preparation for dinner today. Well, I guess there is nothing I can do about it but try to be more careful next time."

He hurried through his mornings preparation and was soon sitting at the table, and talking over the morning's news. For one of the regular duties of his mother was to keep herself posted of the towns happenings . "Allen I see Royal Brinkly is giving a party tonight. I remember when you two, with other boys used to play marbles in the back yard. But, that was before he was sent to private school. Since then you haven't been together much have you, son?"

Watching him as he seemed a little slow in answering, she wondered what had really come between them?

He stared thoughtfully at his plate a moment and replied, "No mother, Royal has grown away from all of his old chums, after his father received an inheritance, he lived in a different kind of world from the rest of us. Instead of playing games as he used to, now, he sits to one side and watches, with an air of importance as though it were far below him to mingle with our class."

His mother proceeded to scan the paper. She turned once more to the local news and commented, "I noticed the housing problem is becoming acute. Here it says, 'there is only sufficient homes for half our population.' and it was only yesterday Sara was telling me she hunted all one day and couldn't find one they could afford to rent, so they made arrangements with her folks for awhile and took the two back rooms of their parents home."

This reminded Allen of the old folks he and Helen had listened to one the day of the wreck.

After telling his mother what they had heard, he discovered he was lingering over his meal too long and began eating.

Now, not able to put the question of houses out of his mind, he stated, "Mother, there are lots of houses empty around here. There's old Ben's place, and old Mrs. Watts has about a dozen over by the ball park. Oh, there's lot of them I could mention but it's no use. What I would like to know is: why those people in the lower end of town live in such tumbled down places when there's so many houses vacant. It looks to me, like something should be done about it. I don't believe they have very much ambition or it's mighty poor management. Say, Mother, how much do they want for a medium-sized house?"

His mother looked up from her paper and replied, "Sara says if she had dealt for any of those she looked at the other day, it would have taken nearly half of Tom's check each month."

The idea of a home costing half of a man's earning came as a surprise to Allen, he considered that he needed to learn more about work and the cost of the things that people needed to live.

Allen's Mother folded up the paper, rose then asked, "What are you going to do today, son?"

Allen changed his trend of thought and replied, "Well, I hadn't thought out the whole day's program, but Mr. Harris wanted me to go with him to get the professor. After that, I don't know. That reminds me, we we're going to the hospital at ten o'clock today. Come on, Mother, let's get the dishes done and I'll run over and see if Mr. Harris is ready to go."

He found that helping his mother with the dishes was now an interesting but a short chore. He soon finished, put on his hat, and called as he left, "See you later."

As he proceeded along the path and out of the gate a feeling of joy filled him. His own whistle became a discord as he stopped to listen to an Oriole who was pouring out its innermost feeling in a song to his mate. He walked on. The flowers seemed to nod a challenge to him for their beautiful colors blended with the blue sky and the freshness of spring.

He watched a pare of humming-birds gathering their fill from a honeysuckle vine. His attention was so focused he did not see Helen coming along the path towards him.

"Caught you napping again." Helen said as she caught him by the arm.

Together they spun around, once, twice, again and again, blood spun to their heads. Their feet seemed to hardly touch the firm earth as the trees and fences flew in arcs about them. Allen's grip slipped. Helen shouted a warning as they slowed to a stop, clinging tightly together they rested as the rest of the neighborhood continued to spin in hectic circles.

Allen, being the first to collect his wits playfully scolded, "You rascal, now we are both drunk. At first it was only drinking in the beauty of spring as I watched our feathery friends enjoy it. But, now, you go so far as to even stagger."

The suddenness of it all took Helen as much by surprise as if that rolling, tumbling world, that seemed so slowly to settle to rest , had stopped and left her at another place on it. Even the trees and bushes seemed to change places. Then slowly they righted themselves and stopped moving as the world came back to normal.

She discovered she was resting most of her weight on Allen by clinging to his arm.

"Let's sit down for awhile, for I surely need to after a fright like that. Say, Allen, what made you act so quickly? I thought I was going to get a joke on you."

They chose a comfortable place where they could watch the honeysuckle vine while they were talking, for Allen wanted to show her the humming-birds.

When seated he replied, "You did, for I didn't know there was a person within a block of me. I was going over to your place to see your father. Is he ready to go?"

Allen noticed the birds were back, he carefully pointed towards the vine, Helen looked up and saw them as she excitedly whispered, "Aren't they cute little fellows? See, they don't even put their feet on the flowers to spoil them, they just flutter above them as if they really appreciated the meal the flower was serving. There comes another one, look, they've got their heads together. I believe, they are really talking to one another. See, they are."

Sure enough they both turned and started on their flight toward a large heavily leafed tree.

Intent on the scene of birds and flowers, they both intently watched the tiny pair until the foliage hid them from view. Helen said, "Yes, father was ready, but the professor called and told him not to come until two o'clock. The doctor is going to x-ray him again before letting him go, he wanted to be sure he was well enough before he left the hospital. Say. Allen, I believe, he's going to be real interesting. Don't you?"

Allen was speculating on what would be best to do with the time, for here it was about ten o'clock. Then he remembered his folly of last night when he spoiled the tarts, replied, "Yes, I do. I believe he and your father will have very interesting discussions, and I sure want to listen to some of them. You're not very interested in such things are you?"

Helen meditated for some time before answering, "Allen, you have touched a very tender spot in our home life. As you know, mother is very religious. She believes we were created in God's image and all things were created for the benefit and use of man. We should first prepare ourselves in this life to return to our maker and live with him. In order to accomplish this we must be punctual at all the services of the church, pay our assessments and tithing regularly, and live to be married for time and eternity. But, father looks at life from a different viewpoint. He, as you know, believes that man is a product of biological evolution.

In the years that I can remember I have never heard them quarrel over this. They made an agreement when they were married that each would believe as they pleased as far as their religion was concerned. And that it should never be brought up as a controversy between them.

Now Allen, I love them both and I try not to show the least bit of partiality between them.

Mother has that tender appealing character that comes by continually striving to perfect herself, through her love for her family she's able to bind us together in perfect unity. She believes that by learning to love one another as God does we can work together and create a world where everyone can enjoy and share in the abundance of God's creations.

Father is of the same loving type, but, has a background of an entirely different kind. He believes, that man has been millions of years in the making. That it has taken the experiences of all those stages of the past animal life, that he sees in the different layers of rocks in the earth, to produce man as he is, a really thinking animal, one who can look back over the ages of time, and really appreciate his position above all other animals.

He believes, that man should unite in a common purpose to protect themselves from the ravages of nature, and build themselves better mentally and physically by having better schools and better methods of teaching.

Especially is he very considerate with children. For he believes, only can these things be accomplish if the children of today are brought to a better understanding of tomorrow.

Mother sees the same fossils as only being in one or two layers of the earth, to her, supporting the Bible history of the flood.

Allen, I tell you these family secrets because father has told me of his offer to you. This will bring you closer to the family, and by knowing it will save us all many embarrassing moments."

As Allen listened, a choking feeling came into his throat. He could see what a blessing she was to the peace of her family.

How clearly she seemed to understand both of them and how she must trust him to be telling him of their intimate family life. He could see that she spoke with a surging inner emotion that almost choked her at times. There was an urge within him to put his arm about her to try to console her.

Her appeal to him seemed to be in the very depths of those blue eyes, then again, it would seem to emanate from her whole being. She finished speaking with a slight catch in her voice and a mist gathering in her eyes, it was more than he could stand. So giving in to this urge, he put his arm around her and as if by a signal, she turned her face towards him. And with a heart felt yearning their lips met in a mutual understanding.

Then feeling as if the curious eye of all nature had been watching their weakness, they blushingly separated from the kiss that had been built up in sympathy and consolation by the ever pressing urge of youth. Self-consciousness had gripped them and was tearing at their hearts with the fear that someone had spied upon them and would turn loose that dreaded dragon of all ages, rumor, which changes the truth to fable as it goes from tongue to tongue.

Not seeing anyone to chide them, Allen quickly spoke, "Helen, I did not mean to embarrass you this way. But it seemed the only way I could show my heart felt sympathy and appreciation of your confidence."

Her eyes looked straight into his, and with note of true affection in her voice replied, "Allen, I believe you. If it had not been so, I could not have responded to your appeal. Come on, let's not be too serious about it for it was a happy moment to us both."

Arising, they were soon smiling and back in their earlier mood of laughing and joking. But suddenly the smile left Allen's face, he had remembered the tarts again.

Helen, saw the quick change and looked sharply around to see what had happened. Not seeing anything she hurriedly asked, "What's the matter?

Is something wrong?"

This brought a guilty flush to his face as he replied, "Not exactly wrong, but hard to explain."

After he told her of his nightmare, he slowly unraveled the story of the cake and tarts.

Helen was dismayed at the story but she playfully took hold of his ear as she replied, "Now my gallant lover, you're going home and help me make some more."

With a grimace as if in pain he protested, "But, Helen, it was a pure accident, besides think of the fear and trembling I received for my pains. Now to be captured and held until I rectify my mistake and repent.

But it's always the same. All conquerors are oppressors while the victims are held by the ear."

Her smile widened out into a good hearty laugh as she gave his ear a slight tweak to even things up a bit.

Then smothering her laughter she assumed a sober face to answer, "I accept your apology. But the insinuation as to my prosecution of innocent victims, I resent. You are still held prisoner until we come before your mother that she might judge the extent of the crime committed.

Soon they Arrived home and brought the question before the judge, and sentence was passed that he should make the tea, set the table, and eat all the broken tarts.

But Helen protested, "I believe, the prisoner incompetent and the labor to his disliking, so I appeal to the judge to allow the prisoner to assume half the burden."

The appeal for leniency was accepted and with merry remarks they began the task at hand.

Allen's mother settled back in her arm chair, watched the joking and laughing pair as they prepared the lunch. Memories of her past girlhood days came back in review to her.

Days she had played with the girls of her age within the neighborhood. She remembered how they were expected to keep themselves isolated from the boys of the village, until she and her girl friends were of sufficient age to have parties with them. Each girl invited her own partner and afterwards was called his girl by the children of the neighborhood. These friendships were broken up by misunderstandings, until she became a young woman. Then she met John.

They had seemed to understand each other from the first, and she had enjoyed those first flirtations at dances, parties and picnics. John had become jealous at times, ending in fighting among the boys. Later they were married.

His father had given him a farm. Where they settled down to work and enjoy life. The horror of war burst forth and the young men of the country were drafted and trained to fight. One day the dreaded letter came, and as it was read a sickening fear clucked at her heart. It was his call to arms. There followed sorrow, tears and a feeling of despair. Many times she heard the tales of war and it's horrors from the lips of her grandfather who was in the Civil War. These stories informed her of the chances of his return.

She took her baby in her arms and longed for something to stop the war before the day he must go. She watched the hours, hating the minutes to pass. Finally the dreaded day came that he had to go, they went to the station together. Many other men and boys of the neighborhood were there. Those being left behind were weeping or trying not to show their true feelings in regard to their hopelessness and doubt.

After she waved a last farewell, she had returned home to wait-- work and wait with an aching heart for his return.

One year had passed and nearly another when an official looking letter came.

Suddenly Allen called, arousing her from her reverie. "Mother, what's wrong? You're crying."

He became much worried and hurried to her side.

His mother in order to stay his fears, answered, "Son, do not be alarmed. I was sitting here watching you two prepare lunch and thinking over the past. I suppose, I became too absorbed in some parts of it."

She arose to her feet, "How are the prisoners coming with the lunch?

I need my cup of tea."

Chapter V

Rivals Meet

While the woman prepared more cakes and tarts, Allen and Mr. Harris left to get the professor.

They waited only a few moments when he was rolled out to the car in a wheel-chair. He recognized Allen and called out, "Hello, there young man, give me a lift. I am still a little bit shaky yet."

Allen helped the professor into the car, he was surprised to see how much he had improved. Once inside and settled comfortably on the seat, Allen turned to Mr. Harris and introduced them. Noticing each give the other a professional scrutiny before speaking, he wondered if this was to be a professional clash or an intimate friendship between them. His fears were only momentary for a smile came to their faces as the professor spoke, "Mr. Harris I am surely glad to meet you."

Shaking hands, Mr. Harris replied, "I have heard of you many times in the past and I am surely glad to have this opportunity to exchange ideas with you."

The professor, feeling this outspoken friendship, replied. "Yes, Mr. Harris, and your work in geology is well-known and will be prized by many generations to come."

Allen saw they had become well acquainted and asked. "Mr. Harris, if you do not mind, I'll drive home while you and Mr. Hopkins talk."

Helen's father seemed well pleased as he changed places to the back seat with the professor. Allen always enjoyed the driving of a good car for he had never owned one, but the neighbors had often called on him to drive theirs. Sometimes for long trips into the hills over very rough roads, other times into the crowded traffic of the city.

These experiences gave him practice in becoming a skillful driver, he could now drive and listen to the conversation of the worldly men in the back seat. He learned as they reminded one another of the work to be done in the near future for the advancement of civilization. He heard them say if improvements to safeguard human life were not soon affected, the destructive changes of nature would creep up to destroy them. Man could only survive if they organized collectively on the basis of labor value.

Then they would be able to meet these changes and carry on as the modern human being with the world at their command.

This seemed all to far advanced in thought for Allen's understanding, he turned his attention to the car, the pleasant purr of the motor was more familiar to him as it moved them along.

When they arrived at home and stopped, the conversation in the back seat still continued, but when he opened the door and slid from behind the wheel they ceased.

With the professor between them, they gave support and made their way to the house. The door swung open for them to enter, Allen's mother, expecting them, had opened it, thinking the professor would need all of them to help.

Once inside Allen began, "Mother, meet Mr. L. T. Hopkins." He was startled by reaction of his mother and the professor.

They did not seem to notice the presence of others as Mr. Hopkins exclaimed, "Why Anne, of all the people I ever expected to meet, you are the last. I had completely lost track of you."

They shook hands as Allen's mother replied with a shocked expression, "Tom, when you went away from the old home, you disappeared. Now this is surely a pleasant surprise. Have you been back lately?

There are so many questions to ask you. Come let's sit down. We seem to have surprised everybody.

I think we had better make this meeting clear to rest. Tom, will you tell them about our childhood days?"

Helen and Allen stood by Mr. Harris, while the professor told the story. "It began away back when we were children. The boys would tease the girls and vice versa. We grew up as the ordinary neighborhood children do to young men and women. Anne chose me as her partner to a community party, or as they're sometimes called, a bazaar. This set us out as sweethearts by the neighborhood young people. Well, we continued to go to parties and then to dances until one day the opportunity came for me to go east to college. This broke up all our future plans for dances and parties. We had a little quarrel but I went in spite of everything. The next news I heard from home was, Anne had married. I changed my name a bit, going by the name of Lenard T. Hopkins, this being the name by which I am known today. In the past ten years I have traveled to about every part of the world. Last month I went back home and looked around and found that everything had changed so much it was not even interesting. So I decided to go to the West Coast for awhile, and here I am."

After a slight pause in the conversation, Helen interrupted, "Come, we have a lunch prepared in the dinning room."

All consenting, they arose as Helen's father exclaimed, "I believe a cup of tea and lunch will make us all feel better acquainted."

Everybody began laughing and joking about the queer things that had happened in their experiences.

After lunch Mr. Harris begged to be excused, "Folks, I will have to go. I have a little writing to do. I promise I will be back with the wife for awhile this evening."

Catching up his hat from the rack he was soon out of sight down the road.

Allen's mother and the professor returned to the dining room while he and Helen cleared the table.

Allen could hear them talking as he helped with the dishes, but when he looked over at Helen, he sensed a seriousness in her sudden change of mood. Determined to break the silence he asked, "Helen, what makes you so moody? Ever since lunch you haven't spoken a word. You can smile and I surely like to see you do that."

Little did he know the thoughts that were disturbing her inner-feelings for the last few moments. As she scanned his features she knew within herself that his advances were sincere and backed by the highest type of friendship. Not a friendship behind which lurked the subtle mind of the gentleman-like hypocrite, or the crude planning of that mental infant of caveman days with it's violent passions of hate and desire-- But a friendship which invites ones innermost confidence and appreciative feelings.

Little had she realized these traits within him in the years past, for had not other young men offered her their friendship and taken her to parties and dances. They were interested in their ideals of life and their individual narrowness in procuring them. One among them had plenty of material means of the world, enough to be a prize desired by most any young woman seeking a social position. He had spent many hours at her home talking to mother and her of the interesting and desirable things in life to be gained by travel or mixing in the upper social levels of society.

Now, since her intimate friendship with Allen a new light had began to shine. One in which a new kind of human understanding had developed within her, opening the way to procure true happiness- not of the narrow property kind, but a comradeship within which she had someone that could work with to help bring to the world the knowledge of a better system of civilization.

With sudden determination, she flashed a smile to him as she spoke, "Allen, I want you to excuse me this evening. I have an invitation to Royal Brinkly's affair and he will be coming over home for me at eight. Therefore, I must leave here by six o'clock to be ready and it is after five now."

His heart sank at the mention of Royal's name. Anguish filled him as question after question filled his mind. The most potent one of all-- why does Royal always appear to interfere with my feelings? This question would flash before his mind, aggrieving his mental condition until it began to show a pained and bewildered expression on his face.

He felt hurt by her not staying the first evening the professor was at his home, she continued, "Royal asked me to accompany him to his party some time ago but I didn't know what day it would be until yesterday when I received the card. Please do not think me a cad, as if I were trying to slough the responsibility or something of that nature, for I really would enjoy staying this evening. There are so many questions I would like to ask the professor, and I believe you and I could help make the evening a success."

Allen had now recovered sufficiently to answer without a show of emotion as he replied, "Helen, I do not question your integrity, but there are other questions which I so not understand. We will not refer to them now for the time is short before you have to go. I believe it would be best, if we let mother and the professor know you will not be here."

As they walked into the living room, they found the professor and Allen's mother still talking of their friends and changes that had taken place in their old home town.

The professor turned to them and asked, "Anne says you sing well, Helen. Will you please sing for me?"

This took Helen by surprise, but as singing was a pleasure to her, she replied, "Yes, I will gladly sing a song or two, but first I will have to tell you, I can't be here for the rest of the evening for I unwittingly made an engagement a week ago for a party, which happens to be tonight. I will return tomorrow because I still have a lot of questions to ask."

She opened the organ cover, then began to sing an old love song. One that touched the very topic the elderly pair had been reviewing.

Allen could see an emotion exciting them as the song told of love with two hearts as one. As jealousy arose between them there came a sad,

sad parting-she with the determination of her kind not to be flung to the winds by one so fickle-he with a feeling as though his character and pride had been trampled on- then years in which to pay for their rash decision but ending with love and lasting friendship.

He could see them live the depths of despair as the song went on to the end. They smiled as it closed with lovers united. He had not missed understanding the story of the professor. He could see the truth of the song Helen was singing, so without attracting notice, he moved closer to the organ, and leaning over he received a knowing wink from Helen.

After the chorus was finished he suggested, "Helen, please play one we can all sing."

She struck up a lively tune, and all were soon singing as though in the best of spirits.

Allen noticed his mother's voice had a full rounded note that had not been there before. She was enjoying every moment as her bosom rose and fell with the effort to express her feelings in the song. Allen could see she was living again those younger days before the cares and heartaches of motherhood and engulfed her.

Allen glanced at the professor, he saw him watching his mother with pride and enjoyment in every expression of his face.

Every one of them had enjoyed those songs, each with their own reasons giving them the satisfaction that the songs were well sung.

Helen excused herself again as she prepared t leave.
Allen, caught her by the arm then called over his shoulder to his mother and the professor, "I'll be back in a minute."

He intended to walk with Helen to her home then run back to make up for his absence.

As they walked along, Helen turned a puzzled face towards him and asked, "Allen how do you feel about the professor?

Do you still think we did the right thing by bringing him to our place?"

He paused in thought a moment before he answered, "Mother is old enough to know her own mind. This afternoon she has shown more expression of pleasure on her face than I have seen in my whole life, with the exception of when she took me on her lap when I was smaller and told me stories. Now that I am grown I do little things just to please her. I believe, she and the professor have a common understanding. I believe we will learn more about it in the next few days.

What do you honestly think about it?"

Helen felt as if a burden had been lifted from her shoulders as he reveled his feelings. As she felt this sudden release she began, "Allen, I've been afraid ever since this visit was first mentioned that there would be something to regret. Not knowing of their acquaintance in the past or your attitude concerning the rumors which are sure to follow. Now I feel as though we were going to be able to talk and act free of what other people might think."

They continued to discuss this subject the rest of the way home.

Little did they foresee the situation that was already developing there.

Royal had come early to talk to her father concerning a contract which he and his father were interested in.

Mr. Harris was sitting back in his chair as he listened to Royal's story. "Mr. Harris, we have been successful in obtaining the contract for the dam in Rollins Canyon, in that we are not sure of the geology of the location we need the advice of a geologist. I told father of your drilling a test hole in the upper valley for oil. He suggested that it might be best to acquire your services, seeing that you already know and have accurate data of this geology, and by so doing we can save thousands of dollars in the dam's construction. We may make the offer very interesting if you will consider it."

Helen's father did not reply at once for he was testing this young man's story from a very different angle, one in which the welfare of hose who were to live below this dam would be considered. He had already investigated the responsibility of the company that was to build the dam under a sub-contract.

"Royal, I am sorry to tell you, my services have already been spoken for. I am now employed by the original contractors. The complete report has already been turned over, samples and test results of the hole we drilled at the narrows was included.

There is one thing I would like to warn you about now. It is nearly a hundred feet down to solid rock in those narrows. The soil formation is of such a nature that a slight seepage of water into it would make that canyon bottom a rolling mass of mud and foam to come roaring down over this very village. Royal, your company's bid was too low to do this enormous amount of excavating to solid rock without cutting immensely on the generally expected overhead or by slighting some of the necessary work to be done.

Short-cuts in a project such as this could result in death of my friends, family and destruction of our homes.

I do not want you to consider me as an enemy but I have other reports to make concerning the escarpment surrounding the dam. I have already an assistant to help me with the test hole up in the valley. With these reports to make my time will be well taken up."

Helen's father then paused to see if Royal wished to carry on the conversation. Instead Royal rose to his feet with an expression of surprise as he answered, "Mr. Harris, I did not expect to meet such a surprise as this enormous depth to excavate, nor did I expect to hear of such a thing as your being already employed in this undertaking. My father will be greatly disappointed in not being able to have your support and confidence. However, I hope we may still get along as friends."

At this moment Helen and Allen were seen coming along the path, and to Royal they appeared to be very interested in the subject they were discussing, illustrated by their smiling faces along with the nods of understanding for extra-expression at intervals making their discussion appear as one that's settled once and for all.

To Royal there seemed to be too much intimacy in that understanding, for he had hoped to win her affection and confidence without the interference of an early rival. As he now watched their slow progress up the path, the show of eagerness in their conversation printed plainly in his mind the picture of defeat. His whole being wanted to cry out in bitter protest. The pounding of blood in his temples made him feel as though every beat of the heart would drive him insane, while in the rest of his body it seemed to run icy and cold. Then came strife within him as the passion of hate brought a curtain of red before his eyes, A convulsion seemed to shake his body as the realization of his weakness dawned upon him. The life of ease he had lived required but little exertion to build the strength necessary to satisfy such a desire as physical revenge.

Suddenly he realized his feelings were showing on his face. With a forced smile and a grim determination he resolved to settle the matter with the means of which he could master.

In order to hide his embarrassment he turned away from the oncoming pair as Mr. Harris began, "Royal, you misjudge me. We do not as yet understand one another."

Turning to Helen and Allen as they came up to them, he continued, "Royal, I expect you know Allen, so meet him as my expected assistant, for he will be working with me in the preparation of data concerning the dam if he accepts."

Chapter VI

Reunion

The suddenness of the introduction by Helen's father, did not upset Royal as much as the announcement of Allen as his assistant. His inner rage griped him again, then subsided as he made his decision concerning Allen. He then turned to Helen and apologized, "Helen, I am not here to rush you to the party, you see, I had a little business with your father. That is now complete, please tell me what time you will be ready, I will call back for you then."

Helen, noticing the coldness he had shown towards Allen hesitated a little before she replied, "I was intending to be ready at eight o'clock, but I am a little late getting home so if you will call back at nine I will surly be ready."

Royal smiled as he thanked Helen's father for his time and consideration, just before he turned to go he paused and as an after thought, began, "Mr. Harris, I am going to bring father out to see you tomorrow so that he can do his own business transactions. That way I'll not be entirely responsible for the outcome, of course, that is if you don't mind."

Helen's father nodded assent as he departed, then turned his attention to his daughter. "Helen, your mother is waiting to see you before we leave for Allen's home this evening."

Helen, curious about what was so important called out as she left to see her mother, "See you tomorrow! Good-night."

Helen's father placed his arm on Allen's shoulder and warned, "I don't believe Royal likes you much judging from his reaction when I told him you are my expected assistant. Never mind, we have a few moments while the ladies get ready for the evening, let's go to the study, sit down and I'll share a little history of the work at hand."

Allen promised his mother he would be right back after he walked Helen home but, he could not disappoint Mr. Harris. So reluctantly he followed him into the library.

Soon he was following the story with much more interest than he would have admitted. The building of a dam is very important to the community and having a part in its construction gave him a thrill of pride.

The older man related the history of the oil well, the narrows where the dam would be built and the valley that would soon be filled with a lake. He was just telling about the valley when the study door swung open and Mrs. Harris called,

"Herbert I am ready to go."

Mr. Harris paused and answered, "All right, dear, give us about five minutes more."

The door closed again as he continued listing the studies .

Five minutes later Helen's mother opened the door again and almost ran into them as they were coming out.

Mr. Harris was adding the last bit of the story when his wife exclaimed, "My goodness, I almost fell into your arms. I thought I would have to remind you again a time or two before yo would be ready to go."

She took hold of her husband's arm and continued. "Now you are started, come along. Don't you know Anne expects us? And they will be wondering where Allen has gone to."

Mr. Harris let Allen know they were finished for now he then went to take care of necessary chores before going out for the evening.

Allen waved to Helen, who was watching from the window as he ran home meaning to make up for his absence.

He stopped at the gate, and wondered if other visitors were there, for he could hear his mother's voice softly harmonizing with the chord of the organ. Her voice carried within it a feeling of rest, motherly love, and happiness. He couldn't remember her singing with such feeling in his short life.

It thrilled him to see her so happy, for he had often wondered what he could do to keep her from brooding and worrying about him all the time.

For a moment he stood and listened, hating to open the door and disturb the peaceful effect of her beautiful song. Slowly he edged toward the door, then waited until the last strains of the music died away. Feeling as though the slightest sound would amplify into an explosion, he slowly turned the knob. When the door gave way, he gazed at a sight to inspire the most hardened desperado. There in the soft fading light sat the professor in a sound peaceful sleep. The restful expression on his face told of his deep pleasure as he enjoyed the strains of soft pleasing music.

His mother didn't notice that he was asleep as her figures turned the pages of music to select another tune. Once selected, her fingers began to touch the keys to create the tune of an old lullaby. Her voice blended in delicate harmony bringing out the words of rest and cheer he had heard many times in his childhood came forth. Then as the song neared the chorus it's appeal won his attention, he moved behind her and enjoyed the soft pleasing strains. As the song ended, he gently put his arm over her shoulder, brushed his face against hers and kissed her on the cheek.

With a slight show of surprise she smilingly turned and patted him on the cheek as she spoke, "Son, you startled me when you put your arm on my shoulder for I did not hear you come in."

She glanced toward the professor and would have continued but Allen gave a nod of understanding and replied, "Mother, I am happy to see you take such an interest in life and I hope you enjoyed your music for it seems more like home, a place to come to not only with trouble and tears but with laughing, and joking, confidence and companionship. Mother I hope you understand me right, for when I came in this evening I felt the thrill of home more than ever before, I am so glad to be here to enjoy it."

The footsteps of Mr. and Mrs. Harris were heard as they came up the walk, his mother quickly arranged the music and stepped to the door to greet them.

Allen noticed the professor starting to wake from the sound of the greetings getting closer and louder. He moved his chair closer to him to relay his warning. "Mr. Hopkins you are caught napping, we have company."

The professor, a little startled, seated himself more erect and apologized, "By George, I must be a baby for your mother was singing a lullaby the last I remember."

Allen remembering how it affects him replied. "Yes, I fall asleep too when I hear these old songs. This is the first time mother has sung in years."

When the other three joined them Mr. Harris ceased jollying Allen's mother, took his wife by the hand and continued jokingly, "Meet Anne's old friend, Mr. Hopkins, please don't keep him too busy answering questions for I have a very important problem upon which I would like his opinion."

Mrs Harris laughingly let it pass for a joke as she exclaimed, "Very well then Mr. Hopkins, we will get to the questions some other time. Now don't you two men spend all the evening on your discussion, for Anne and I will need some of your attention too."

She remembered with a sudden thought that they had left Allen's mother standing alone during this introduction. Looking around the room in quest of her she found her busily rearranging the flowers in the window sill.

She hurried over to her and exclaimed, "Anne, there is so much to talk about I hardly know were to start."

She saw that Anne was trimming a new species of flowers, one she had never seen before. So for a short time their discussion centered on it's adaptability to the climates of different parts of the world. Then the conversation changed to other subjects of particular interest to women.

Allen listened to the professor, and Mr. Harris talk over the problems of the dam's construction. The need to move one hundred feet of soft material and anchoring the foundation into bedrock, but then their conversation consisted of mostly technical terms, so he soon lost interest and turned his thoughts to his own problems.

Should he accept the responsibility of the work Mr, Harris had offered him?

He felt he could think it over better if he were out in the fresh air so he sauntered into the kitchen and out the back door.

The evening air was filled with the perfume of spring flowers, their fragrance enticed him on until he forgot the problem at hand.

In his desire to cast aside the fatigue of the evening, he walked briskly then finally ran until exhaustion forced him to sit down to rest.

Royal could hardly control his feelings of hate and discouragement in his none too gracious stride to the car. The unsatisfactory answer from Mr. Harris came with a touch of irony. He contemplated how the victory of his father getting the contract was now overshadowed by the financial burden of the additional costs involved in constructing the dam right. The hate, disappointment and discouragement raged within him as he raced his car the twenty miles home.

On arriving home Royal rushed to his father's study in hopes of finding him in. No! he was not there. His heart sank within him as he rushed through the house questioning all that he met. His footsteps faltered as he went to the divan and collapsed into it. He had to regain his composure after Mr. Harris gave him one disappointment after another, to make the moment even more unbearable, jealousy and hate had consumed nearly all his remaining strength.

He became alert as he heard a gruff voice. "Where is he?"

His father came into the room, a well-groomed man about fifty years of age. His cold flashing eyes peered through the fog of cigar smoke to find his son slumped on the divan. He moved to his side and asked, "Son, what is the matter, are you hurt or sick? You look pale."

Royal took a moment to partially regain his self-control before answering, "Father, I am sorry, but now the cat is out of the bag. Harris has already sold to the Bergus Group. Worst of all I have the lowdown on the dam site, it's awful. According to his drilling report there's a hundred feet of dirt and silt before we get down to solid rock. Our contract calls for the concrete to be poured on a solid rock footing.

No wonder that Bergus gang let us have the contract and tied us up so solid. I believe they did it to move us out of the way. Father, we're not able to excavate a hundred feet deep. It will break us flat."

His father sat puffing his cigar listening until he finished. Then with a consoling voice replied, "Royal, it looks like the big boy has us sewed up tight, but, we might find a way out yet.

He wouldn't listen to your money proposition then?"

He glanced at Royal with a sullen expression as Royal exclaimed: "No"

"Well, son, you like this girl of Harris's do you not?"

Royal moved uneasily,

"Do you think that with her as your partner, you could handle this situation to our advantage?

If so, why not get busy winning her over?

I believe you could do it easily."

Patting him on the back as he arose to walk around the room a few times, he consoled, "Royal, think it over, but don't get too sentimental, Win her over strictly to benefit the business, and the company will back you to the limit."

This was a new angle, he turned it over and over in his mind then an enthusiasm gripped him. He could picture her giving in to his persistent wooing when he applied the tricks of romantic conquest that he learned by experience over the last few years. His confidence was high because of his many successes in the past. Now with renewed energy and purpose he sprang to his feet and replied, "Father, I'll do my best, what luck! I have a date with her, she is to be my partner at the party tonight. Gee, it's half past eight now and I promised to meet her at nine."

He Stepped closer to Royal, trembling with pleasurable appreciation for his son's ambition and cooperation as he added with encouragement, "My boy, you are doing fine, all you need now is to just apply what you learned to accomplish our purpose. I have a man waiting for me in the library, well good luck, I'll see you latter."

Royal ran to his car, for now he would have to drive fast to be there at nine o'clock. Excitedly he started the motor and as if impatient the big car lurched ahead as the rear wheels spun, throwing a cloud of dust far out behind. Each revolution of the tires forced the heavy car ahead faster and faster. At seventy miles per hour the buildings and trees slipped by like a blur. The intervals between the objects grew shorter and shorter then blending into a solid line as the car pitched to eighty miles per hour.

Royal could feel his strength come back to normal, the muscles in his body grew tense as if in preparation to meet something unexpected.

Speeding had always brought a thrill of enjoyment to him refreshing memories of the times he had taken girls for a spin at first they were frightened then pleasure caused the color to return to their faces.

It was like using wine to break down the barrier of formality to make it easy to talk and understand each other. Once the barrier was down he could bring the evening to a close with success. He Slowed down to normal speed when he turned the corner to Helen's home. He could see the house and hoped she was ready because he didn't want to meet her father again tonight.

At last he turned up the driveway toward the house, his heart sank, for there was not a light to be seen. Suddenly Helen came out of the front door and ran down to the car.

"I thought you weren't coming, and I had about given up waiting, so I turned out the light and was just going to bed when I heard the car coming up the driveway. What was the matter? You said you would be here at nine o'clock."

Royal glanced at his wrist watch before answering. What met his gaze forced a groan past his lips as he asked, "What time is it? My watch said eight-thirty when I left home, and that is what it says now."
He held his arm out to prove to her that he was telling the truth.

"It is about nine-thirty now, so I guess it's too late to worry about a party. Especially one twenty miles away, so let's call it off."

"This brought Royal out of the car and on to his feet as he pleaded, "Helen, don't let me down like this, for I have a party going on at home and by now they are impatiently waiting for us to get there. Honest, I was misled by my watch or I would have been here earlier."

Then taking her hand he renewed his pleadings, "Run and get your coat, while I turn around for we will have to hurry or they will give us up as a bad job and go home."

Helen yielded, for his pleadings seemed to be sincere, "Alright, I will go, but remember, I have to be home by twelve-thirty."

Royal breathed a sigh of relief when she consented. He had become worried for fear that she would not go. In a moment's time the car was turned around and Helen was ready to go. They were off like a flash, he intended to be at the party at ten o'clock to get the other results he expected.

Helen responded to the speed of the car as most others had. At the end of the journey Royal looked at his watch, for he started it before he left Helen's home, now it was five minutes to ten.

"Well, I don't know how correct this time is, but it only took us twenty-five minutes to get here.

How's that for moving along?

Do you like to ride fast?"

Helen with a flushed face and an excited tremor in her voice replied, "I was just spell-bound by the way things seemed to pass us."

Helen staggered a little because the unaccustomed high speed left the queer sensation that the world was still moving under her feet.

Royal took advantage of this by slipping his arm around her waist and appeared to stagger too. This made them an awkward looking pair as they held to each other for support.

Chapter VII

Party Experience

The party was progressing exceptionally well, for Royal's mother took care of the affairs immediately when he left to pick up Helen. When they entered the beautifully decorated ballroom, Helen saw it would be different than any party she had ever been to before.

As the dancers were carried along by the rhythmic appeal of the dance, she could feel herself elevated into a world where jolly groups of young people moved from place to place gaily seeking their fill of the evenings pleasure.

The guests revolved about the hall talking, joking or drinking as they forced each other to the limit in gaining the most for themselves from the evenings entertainment. They were only there a few moments when they were noticed by many of the guests and a general tumult started. Most of them had missed Royal, though his mother had promised he would be back a little latter in the evening.

With an apology he twisted Helen to a willing young men and skillfully began to direct the evenings pleasures into more concordant lines of thought and actions. He hoped to make this a night of hilarity, one of the prominent affairs of his set that would not be forgotten.

As the confusion increased it became apparent that the young women were not receiving her "with open arms," because their male companions were beginning to "eye her up" as a prospective dance partner. This meant that many of the males would soon become enthusiastic in their efforts to entertain Royal's "New Girl."

While she danced about the spacious hall with her many partners, Helen wondered at the expense that must be met in such a mansion where the ballroom included such furnishings with the background of paintings and architecture. It made her feel as though they were mingling with the social elite, who were called together by kings and queens.

The evening wore happily on until she became aware that the music had not ceased playing since their arrival. The music was blended from one popular tune to the other gradually increased it's tempo, bringing about a higher pitch of excitement among the guests. She scanned each face as they passed, noticing they were living in a life of higher ambition, hope and desire than she. One that drove them into untold limits of enthusiasm and emotion if not intoxication.

She compared this life of pleasure and excess with hers in the quiet village. She saw that a driving force was carrying, almost forcing them on to greater excesses. Each tune needed something more to entice them on in their ever growing ambition to dance. Each hour needed it's extra stimulant to bring up more energy to continue a night of hilarity that would be remembered in every social whirl.

She realized the need to rest from all of this exertion so with many excuses to her partner she moved away from the crowded ballroom and out in the open air. She let out a sigh of relief as she dropped upon a bench to sit and meditate on how so many had to struggle while others lived without worries for the basics of life.

Many couples were walking in the cool air to relieve their overwrought nerves, or to console a throbbing head. Now once-in-a-while among them lovers could be seen, whose emotions were driving them on to a more serious part of their life.

A young couple who seemed blinded to everything except themselves wandered toward her. Helen did not know what to do, a feeling came over her to run away, but better judgment prevailed.

What would they think of her scampering away alone at their approach?

So she decided to stay and be silent at all costs. Their conversations seemed to center on one certain person who had come in their way.

Their speech was not entirely audible at first, but as they came closer their words became more distinct.

Helen became alarmed again, for it looked as though it was the very bench she was sitting on is the one they decided to use. No, they moved to the grass to rest and talk as they sat closely together with their backs toward her. Now they were more careful not to raise their voices for they nodded and spoke in a whisper, cuddled snugly up to each other and happily embraced. Helen began to feel like an eavesdropper, and as such was thoroughly ashamed. She decided to make a bold front of it and leave when they arose to their feet and with one last embrace, directed their steps toward the ballroom. As they passed under the light Helen caught glimpses of their features she was startled that the young man was Royal, deciding not to be caught in such a trap again, she followed them into the hall.

Royal turned away from the girl and stood near the door talking to friends as he nervously looked about. He didn't see her at first, but as his shifting eyes caught sight of her, he immediately excused himself from the group.

He smilingly advanced toward her as he spoke, "Helen, I have tried to find you for the last half hour, you seemed to have disappeared. Where have you been hiding yourself?"

Without a pause or consideration she replied, "I felt a little tired so I stepped outside for a few moments for a breath of fresh air, so now I feel much better.
What time is it?

I see many of your friends have left for home."

Royal worriedly glanced at his watch, but too quickly to see the hands on the smooth dial, as though startled he answered, "Good night! Helen, it's two o'clock, and I promised I would have you home by twelve-thirty. I'll get your wraps and we'll leave."

Helen felt as though she had overdone the evening. What would her mother think? She consoled herself with the value of the experience and pleasure gained then hurried to meet Royal, who was coming with her coat.

Smiling, he held it for her as he spoke, "Helen, you had better put on your coat, it might be a little chilly out."

She smiled, "No, I'll not put my arms in it, just put it over my shoulders, for I believe it will be warm enough in the car, and I like the feel of this spring air."

Royal ushered her out of the big hall and into his car.

The soothing purr of the motor drew her attention to the masterful way he handled the controls of the car. It gained momentum without the least feeling of effort. He shifted into high gear and unconsciously placed his arm over her shoulders.

A slight tension of resentment met his advance as he voiced his words in a quiet soothing manner, "Did you enjoy the evenings entertainment or was it too many hours of merriment? It appears to have tired you out."

He increased the pressure of his arm to bring her nearer to him.

"No, I feel fine except that I fear the folks will have been worried with my belated home-coming especially at this time of the morning."

The car drifted steadily along, while he talked in a soft pleasing voice of the most interesting events of the evening. He slipped the coat from her shoulders. Soft soothing fingers edged toward the warm tempting curves of her neck, that became more exposed as her head tilted back and her eyes slowly closed in sleep.

He felt the muscles in her neck and arms slowly relax as she settled restfully towards him. His hands smoothed out the collar trimmings that adorned her dress as he felt the slow methodical rise and fall of her bosom. Her flesh was warm and firm as he placed his hand softly on her neck while loosening the binding folds of the gown.

Slowly he swung the car over to the side of the road, easing the big car to a stop without a jar or murmur.

Royal placed his face to hers and kissed her, while he drew her body closer to him.

Helen's eyes gradually opened as she felt the hot breath on her neck. Tingling with new sensations she sat helpless while hands smoothed her body into passiveness.

A roar suddenly broke the silence as a speeding car passed by.

Her dormant senses responded with a sudden lunge that freed her from his grasp, with pleadings and promises he tried to persuade her, but with no avail.

Each second seemed an hour as she pleaded and begged for him to be reasonable, and come to his senses.

Her defense only intensified his desire--a beastly desire that consumed his self control and broke lose in physical rage. He began to tear the clothes from her body.

With clenched fists she beat him in the face until lights began to gleam along the oiled road and dance crazily up and down as a car came closer. The light played in through the windshield and upon the nude form of Helen as she wrenched herself from his grasp. A scream was stopped by his hand clasped over her mouth but not soon enough, for the brown steely eyes of Allen had seen the struggling nude form with its frightened expression. He saw it was Royal Brinkly's car so he pulled over to the side of the road, leaped to the ground, grasped the door and jerked it open.

Helen screamed as Royal's hand slipped from her mouth.

Allen's muscles instinctively tightened as he sprang forward, seized Royal by the collar and dragged him out o f the car.

Over and about they rolled with flying fists beating each other with the greatest effort. Legs scraped the earth, stirring it into a cloud of dust. In frantic efforts they surged from side to side each straining to gain a position of advantage.

He could feel Royal weakening as he hit him again and again on his cursing lips. He twisted in agony as he tried to brake from Allen's grasp. Momentarily he relaxed then lunged with one last effort and forced his head close to Allen's arm.

A sickening chill went through him as Royal's teeth sank into his flesh. The agony of the moment paralyzed his muscles so they would not respond for a moment. Then he saw Royal's hand slide into his pocket and out. Fearing he had a knife, like a flash he grasped his maimed arm, jumped to his feet yanking the teeth from the flesh of his arm.

Royal rose to meet him, his own rage increased. Allen now violently pounded and beat the face before him, until a painful sigh passed from his lips and his legs crumpled letting him slump awkwardly to the ground.

Allen glanced passed the unconscious figure before him and saw Helen sitting on the fender of the car sobbing. She had put on her coat and was holding a piece of her torn dress to her face.

She arose, dried her tears and quickly ran to his side as she spoke, "Allen, I don't know how to thank you for helping me escape from this scheming madman. I hope you will believe me, when I tell you I was innocently involved in that shameful scuffle, and it was against my will, take me home, Allen, and I will tell you how it came about."

Allen picked Royal up from the ground and packed him to the car, the thought of leaving him lying there unconscious on the road smote his heart.

A flutter came to his eyes and they finally came open.

Helen switched on the dome light exposing a badly beaten face with eyes that stared with fright at the sight of Allen.

When he became more conscious the stare in his eyes turned to an expression of hate, verbally expressed as he regained his voice. " You cheap tagtail. We'll meet again under more favorable circumstances."

Then turning to Helen he continued, "I'm sorry I had to pull that kind of stuff on you, I am driven by forces you would not understand. Leave me here. I'll be all right in a little while, then I'll drive home."

As Allen listened hate welled up for Royal, but even at that, these outspoken feelings made him appear, even when losing, that he was a good sport.

Allen took Helen by the arm helped her to the seat beside him and started the car.

Her heart ached as she thought of telling him such a beastly story. The truth would have to be told for him to even believe her innocent, or help to corroborate her story to the folks.

She began with the whirl of enthusiasm in the ballroom Then with a query, "Allen, have you ever been to a party of socially prominent people. One where they are striving in their entertainments to out-do every social accomplishment of the past?"

She paused as Allen answered, "No, I haven't."

"Well Allen, I don't believe I can explain the grandeur of that ballroom, for every part blended into the mood of the evening. The music never stopped but gradually raised their emotions to the highest pitch of excitement before the evening was over. Tired of this, I went outside to rest and breath a little fresh air. I found a bench and sat down.

There were many others wandering about in the cool air of the gardens. Two of them, a man and a women, came over close to me and sat down on the grass they were plotting against someone, but I didn't hear her name. They were going to use her to gain aid in some financial venture. Once the discussion was settled they began to renew their friendship in loving embraces which made me ashamed to stay longer, and eavesdrop. Then just as I started to rise, to pardon myself, and leave, he exclaimed, 'My, I nearly forgot I had better take her home.' They hurried to their feet and left for the ballroom. I recognized it was Royal as they passed through a beam of light. Once inside I met Royal who was looking nervously around the ballroom apparently for me. He acted like he just noticed the time was two o'clock, then mentioned that we needed to come home.

The quiet purring of the motor has a lulling effect, and I suppose, I lost control and went to sleep. I awoke and discovered Royal with his hand down the neck of my dress, it took a moment or two to collect my senses.

I became angry, refusing with my whole being to submit to such a sneaking method of attach. He tried first to persuade me to submit to a mutual desire, then he offered me money. My anger was mixed with fear as I began to beat him in the face. He responded by threatening me with force, then he tore my clothes off me while I tried to free myself from him.

At times I would push him away and try to open the door, but they must have been locked with a safety catch that I tried to manipulate. But, before I could get the door opened he would catch hold of me again. He was in the act of tearing the last bit of lingerie from off me when you came."

She looked up into his face with a pleading note in her voice then continued, "Allen, I have told you about all I can remember of this awful affair tonight, if there is anything I have missed, I will tell you later."

She stared silently ahead for a moment before continuing, "Oh, don't you believe me? I know the folks will not understand."

Allen knew he could not explain his feeling as he drove the car, so he came to a stop at the side of the road, he held out his hand and said, "Pal, let's shake hands on it. Swallow that lump that's in your throat and listen for a few minutes. I sat listening last night to the professor and your father as they talked of this technicality and that, until I became tired. Then I slipped out the back door for a walk. When I returned someone called for your father and took him with them.

Now it was my duty to take your mother home when she was ready. We all talked, sang a few songs, played cards without thinking of the time. Finally someone glanced at the clock and it said it was one-thirty. Everyone seemed overawed to think so much time had slipped by without it being noticed. Your mother became worried for fear you had come home and was still waiting for your parent's return.

It was about two o'clock when we reached your place. When I started to put the car away, your mother called, 'Come in before you leave. I want you to try my cake.'

I closed the garage door then went towards the house, when she came out all excited exclaiming, 'Allen, Helen is not home yet. I am afraid something has happened maybe the car has wrecked, or even worse.'

Well, I tried to console her with the thought, that you might have become tired, and sat down in some other part of the house and fell asleep. When we looked all through the house and didn't find you I thought sure your mother was going to faint. So I suggested that she go back home with me, then I would come to town and see what had happened. Finally I persuaded enough that she consented, now she is at my place with my mother."

Allen stopped talking as he noticed Helen's worried expression. With real wonderment he asked, "What is the matter?"

Helen's voice choked as she replied, "What do you think I should tell mother about tonight's tardiness?

I hate to tell her all that has happened for several reasons. She is so devoted to her belief that it is her duty to carry burdens until full payment is made in repentance, to even think such a thing has happened, will only add more burden on her conscience. Her heart has been ailing for some time so she is not very strong.

The other thing is she thinks so much of Royal, I really hate to bring all this trouble onto her at once."

A feeling of sincere responsibility burdened him at the thought of her plight, for it would be very hard to explain ones coming home at this time of the morning under such circumstances. With a firm resolve to see her through he suggested, "Let's hurry home where you can get some clothes first, then, I believe, it will be best to talk with your father when he comes home."

With her nod in agreement, he started the car towards home.

Chapter VIII

A Slight Deception

It was near sunup when Allen drove to the garage and stopped. With a pat on Helen's cheek he reminded, "Now, hurry and we will go over to my place and have breakfast."

She flashed him a smile of appreciation, which drew his eyes to follow her until she disappeared within the house.

He leaned back feeling the support of the seat, his thoughts drifted back over what he had witnessed. Turning each detail over in his mind carefully, the one detail which stood out from the rest Royal's apology to Helen.

What forces were driving him?

Was someone forcing Royal to compromise Helen?

But what for?

What did Helen have to do with the plot she overheard to get financial gain?

All these questions did was bring-up more questions. Then with a firm resolve to find out, he dropped his head back on the seat. This jarred him back to consciousness for he had nearly fallen asleep.

The sound of someone walking up behind he car drew his attention to Helen's father hurrying up behind him. Fear seized him for the moment because now he would have to be the one to break the news.

He saw Allen as he reached the car, so he opened the door and asked, "Did you find her?"

Allen nodded in the affirmative so with relief he continued, "My, I was worried. I came home and everyone was gone, the beds had not been used and the car was gone. So I hurried over to our place only to find both women worried to death, even the professor was all upset. I stopped only long enough to console them, then I hurried back home hoping I would find her here ahead of me. Come in I want to talk to you both."

Allen sensed the tension as he followed him into the house. He wondered if the excitement of the morning had placed him in a bad light in Mr. Harris' opinion of him?

They went into the kitchen and where arranging chairs and were about to sit down when Helen came in.

Her father quickly asked, "Helen, did you have any trouble? My I am glad you are not hurt."

Then he noticed a scratch on her cheek, with concern he continued, "You did have trouble. There, sit down, and tell me all about it."

Helen quickly kissed him on the cheek as she began, "Father, my story may sound flat, for it happened so fast I remember it as only a blur. All I ask is that you believe it to be true. Yes, this morning I did have trouble of a very serious nature, and if it had not been for Allen's timely arrival, I don't know how it would have ended."

She told her father the story of her adventure, Allen watched his hands clinch tighter until the nails were about to cut into the flesh. When she came to the part where he and Helen decided not to say anything to her mother until they advised him, a cloud of thought seemed to pass over his face.

Mr. Harris gazed into the distance as Helen continued with the hope he would start listened to her again, but to no avail. She stopped and touched his arm to draw his attention.

Suddenly he turned and exclaim, "Your mother would never forgive such an act of deception. Of course, her health is of first consideration, she may worry herself sick. So, for the time being, you've had a car accident. Now, while you were talking, Royal's whole scheme flashed through my mind. Now, let me begin at the first.

About a year ago the Bergus Construction Company sent me a letter, inquiring if we still had the log of the well that we had capped at the mouth of Rollins Canyon. I returned the answer that I had. Then about six months later Mr. Bergus himself came to see me.

We took a trip over the field, talking of it's adaptability for a dam site and the possibility of the money being appropriated for it's construction. He made me, what I thought was a good offer, so I accepted. I turned over to him the well log with the understanding I would provide him a complete report of the site's escarpment.

This last is one of the jobs we are working on at the present time."

Looking directly at Allen he continued. "I need your help, Allen, for there are many other investigations I have to complete this summer. Well, back to the story. Well, Royal always did like Helen."

This straightened her up in the chair and drew a determined expression on her face, making it very plain to him that her friendly relations with him had ceased.

Mr. Harris continued, "From childhood days up till now, there has been many interesting visits by him. Now, lately since he went to college, he has been more determined than ever to crowd himself upon me.

He has even deceived mother by making her believe he was interested in my work in geology. Well, when he came out here to enlist me in their adventure of building the dam, he depended on the past friendship of the family to gain the information he desired. With money he intended to involve me into their scheme of beating the public, by cheating in the dam's construction. Then when I refused, and told him of my contract with Bergus, he rushed home, and plotted with his father to gain my support by subjecting Helen to their will. Such a rotten method is very often used in business these days. Say, you two are nearly asleep. Helen, get those trout from the back porch and we'll go over to Allen's for breakfast.

A new light came into their eyes with the mention of trout for breakfast. Both rose simultaneously to get them, as Mr. Harris directed, "I'll be with you in a minute, take them out to the car."

Helen reached them first, for Allen had stopped to listed to her father's wishes, she picked one up by the tale and stated, "This doesn't look like a trout."

Just then it gave a big flop, jerking itself from her hand. A look of surprise and then pain crossed her face.

Allen came fast for blood was beginning to drip from her fingers to the floor. "What did it do? A fish can't bite."

He examined her hand to see where the skin had been punctured in several places.

"They may not be able to bite, but that one must have something sharp to dig holes in my hand so quick, say does that smart," exclaimed Helen.

Allen stooped to pick it up then turned it over to see the fins better, pointed out, "No wonder, look, every fin has three or four needles sticking out from them. Wow, look here at the gills, gosh, he sure is a tough customer to handle. Say, he looks like a bull-head. You remember, the little fellows that used to go like a flash whenever we would go wading in the creek."

Just then her father came in and seeing the commotion asked, "What's all the fuss?"

Then noticing Helen's hand, he exclaimed, "Don't you know a

catfish when you see one?

I forgot to tell you there's three of them mixed in with the trout, are they still alive? They usually live several hours after they have been caught, let's see, Jay took them out of the tank about three hours ago. Come on, it's getting late, we won't get them cleaned in time for breakfast."

Allen tipped the pan and with his foot flipped the not-so-funny prize into it as Helen washed and took care of the bleeding holes in her hand.

"Now that was easy wasn't it?

I waited, thinking there would be some fun, watching you pick it up. Now, I'm disappointed." Stated Helen's father just before he went out to start the car,

At the sound of the cars motor Helen rushed Allen "Hurry, father has the car started."

On a run they went, for Helen's father made as if to leave them. They caught-up and jumped into the back seat.

Helen joked, "If you had left us, we'd have had plenty of fish for breakfast." Then winking at him, "Wouldn't we Allen."

He blushingly replied. "Well, maybe your father would have come back if he'd thought we would fix breakfast."

Helen's mother hurried out to meet them with tears of joy streaming down her face when she saw they coming.

Helen jumped from the car and hugged her and asked, "What are you so exited about?"

Her mother was so choked up with happiness at seeing her, that it was several moments before she could answer. Then with a tremor in her voice she replied. "Dear, I was so upset when I didn't find you home, I went all to pieces.

What was the matter?

My, Goodness it's after sunup, and I'll bet you haven't had a wink of sleep."

Helen laughingly replied, "Oh, yes I have, there was some car trouble and while it was being repaired, I had a rest. It was nearly morning before we left the party, and say, there must have been a thousand people there. Anyway, let's talk about it later. Father's caught some fish and he suggested we fry them for breakfast, What do you say?"

She gathered her mother by the arm and hurried her into the house.

Allen glanced over at her father as he climbed from the car and received an acknowledging look and a sigh of relief in return as he prepared to alight.

Everyone had taken on new life at their return and it was only a few minutes work before the fish were frying in the pan Soon they were talking and sharing many a funny repast.

Once breakfast was finished everyone seemed ready to lean back in their chairs and philosophize on what the summer would bring for them in the way of improvement to the community and the political economy of the nation as a whole.

Finally the professor came forth, for this was his pet topic, "The necessary changes in the politic for our government at the present time are absolutely ignored. Nearly everyone has the idea that prosperity is something to be depended on. That never again would there be a time when this country's thousands, yes, it's millions of hungry families would cry up to it's president, for relief from the political ills that are starving them to death.

The system of distribution in this, like nearly every other country, depends entirely on the basis of profit and private property. The time will come, when the starving millions will assert their right, and rebuild this country on the basis of production and distribution, for all will be workers alike."

Mr. Harris listened with intense interest as the professor expounded his theory of government, several questions of importance crossed his mind so when the professor finished speaking he queried, "At the present time 'the boom is on' so we all seem to have a feeling of security. We trust that we will secure a position of wealth and importance from the grace of an unknown friend. So we continue to accumulate so-called wealth like, bonds, stocks, mortgages, etc. But instead of giving us wealth they are spreading their sucking tendrils into every branch of community life.

I believe, the time will come when all means of livelihood, except the labor which produces it, will be sucked up and controlled by those with whom we entrusted our government affairs until even our government itself will be dictated by them. So, there are several questions of importance that I would like to talk over, which take into consideration the problems of our everyday life. For instance, the dam to be built in Rollins Canyon, Do you think the economic welfare of the people here will improve by it's construction?"

The professor took a moment to consider Mr. Harris' question for a moment and thoughtfully replied, "The availability of water always makes a difference, the holding of the flood water to serve in the dry months will improve the lives of both the farmer that can apply it to more land and the city dweller that can depend on a continuous supply for his endeavors. Then on the other hand new fees and taxes may rob both the farmer and city dweller of these very benefits that they hope to obtain."

These concepts and many others of the same magnitude were discussed with an understanding between them that would make their friendship a bond for life.

Helen and Allen listened with interest until they began to nod off. Then without too much ado they quietly stepped out the door into the fresh invigorating air.

"Whew, I was nearly asleep when you nudged me. If I'd been caught by either your father or the professor, sitting there asleep, I sure would have felt cheap for they were really in earnest and enjoying each others views of the present and future of the country. Say, I've a notion to take your father up on the deal he offered me a few days ago. There is only one part about it, I don't like so well."

Wrinkling his brow to make it appear very serious he continued, "I wouldn't be home very much of the time, at lease, not this summer and I believe I would be missing a lot of good times, with someone, that could help me make life worth living."

Helen's expression changed from one of seriousness to a tantalizing smile as she spoke, "Oh, I see. Is my great big boy worried for fear he will get lost in this great big world of ours?

Now don't be afraid, I'll be around there once in awhile to make it more miserable for you fellows. Father allows me to help him once in awhile. But, I suppose I would only be in the way of two big men if I was around the camp very much of the time."

Allen uplifted by the knowledge that he would see her now and then questioned, "Now, see here, young lady, after all we might as well get serious.

Do you mean to tell me that that you would come out to camp once in awhile and give us real home-cooked meal?"

He wondered if she would enjoy it as much as her eyes were telling, when her voice interrupted, "Here are the cold facts to be met, to work with father is hard work. The day is from sunup to sundown, that is when there is special work to be done. Long hikes and sometimes heavy packs of fossil are the ordinary routine of the day, and sometimes it's very dangerous traveling. OK, let's not pick out all the faults and not mention the good qualities too. First there is plenty of good fresh air and exercise, next, scenery by the hundreds of miles, and let's not forget the cool shady groves of trees along the creeks where one can sit and watch the nearly endless variety of birds, animals, bugs and fishes go by.

Say, don't you get hungry!

When you get to camp just the thoughts of bacon and eggs, mulligan stew made from the wild meats of the hills or fried wild chicken with mushroom sauce gives you plenty of energy to complete the meal without the thought of being tired. Oh, I nearly forgot sleep! One just shuts their eyes and suddenly they open again with a new day dawning. Allen, you would really enjoy it. For I know, when I'm there, I surly do."

At first she nearly took his breath away, for the responsibility of such a day's work he had never had, but the pleasing effect of the mountain scenery and wild life had always furnished the urge to again return, investigate and appreciate nature's innermost secrets. Helen's encouragement was carrying him on to a greater ambition and a better appreciation of the work itself. With the help of her father, he would be able to gain a better understanding of life and the history of it.

This spurred him on as he replied, "With your promise that you will come out to camp once in awhile and help break the monotony, I will accept."

With the promise duly recognized, arm in arm they returned to the house.

Helen's father was first to see that they had some things to tell, nodded to the professor a warning then stopped the conversation momentary, to see what was going to happen.

Allen didn't hesitate as he addressed Mr. Harris, "Helen and I have been talking over the offer you made me the other day, and with mother's permission I will accept."

Then he turned to see his mother's face.

She exclaimed, "Why, Allen, you will be away."

Then she remembered they talked it over once before, she continued, "Son, it may be for the best that you be where you can come in contact with the world and it's problems. I believe, that under the guiding hand of Mr. Harris, you will be able to acquire an education more fundamental to your life than can be gained at school."

These words were spoken with a consoling voice, while within, the idea of his leaving was consuming most of her energy in an effort of self control.

Mrs. Harris noticing this, heartily joined in, "Yes, Anne, I have let Helen go many times with her father, just for the vacation. I noticed each time that she goes she gains a better understanding of the beauty of life. I also believe, it is those trips to the mountains that furnished the proper materials and exercise to make her as healthy as she is. Last summer I had an awful time keeping her home. She wanted to be with her father every minute where she could see and study in nature rather than stay in town."

Allen's mother began to feel better as Mrs. Harris told of letting her only living child go on such excursions, especially so when the thought struck her that he, being a boy, was better adapted to meet the conditions to be encountered.

It was at this point in her reflections that Mr. Harris spoke, "Anne, I realize your anxiety for your son's safety should be acknowledged, for it has taken years of hard work and worry for you to raise the boy we see, as Allen, today. We all recognize his efforts to try and repay that debt, both by his attentiveness to you and his willingness to assume his responsibility and look out for your comforts."

They all seemed satisfied that Allen had taken the proper course, as they gave brief warnings and plenty of encouragement for his chosen adventure into the whirl of business life.

He Glanced at his wife, and then at the clock before Helen's father remarked, "My, it's been many hours since any of us have had sleep. So, I suggest we go home and continue our visit tomorrow."

His wife quickly assenting, procured her wraps and with a grateful attitude, thanked Mrs. Rodak and her son for their help in her time of trouble.

Helen Pinched Allen on the arm to draw his attention, then led the way outside to the car, where she spoke with downcast head and a mist gathering in her eyes, "Allen, I want to thank you for your trust in me, and for that outburst of self determination which saved me from Royal's disgraceful attempt to humiliate and abuse me."

Hearing the folks coming up to the car behind her she hurriedly continued, "Come over in the morning, early. I want to go for a walk and talk to you."

Chapter IX

The Spirit of Adventure

Twenty years ago, the little town of Pospur didn't appear to have the qualities of progress that would soon expand it's homes across the gently rolling surface of Rollins Canyon. Forward thinking men in the community worked to bring it out of it's early morning dreamy mood and bring about prosperity.

"Water" had been the cry of every progressive individual that had investigated it for a home.

"If we could only get more water, this would be the most fertile stretch of ground within many miles." Was the conclusion that many had come to.

With this fact to continually remind them of it's necessity, the town inhabitants organized a company to build a canal from Rotan Lake to Pospur. Everyone in town took a keen interest in this prospect, if such a venture were to succeed they would all reap the benefits.

With the hope of getting water many acquired a portion of the bench land, which, in the past, had only been of use for early pasture. These invested in the newly organized company in hopes of increasing the value of their bench lands. Soon happy groups of jostling men, with their horses and equipment, were making their way to the lake to begin the project. After several years of toil, bankruptcy, and heartaches it was completed. To their disappointment it was only partially able to supply the water needs of all those that invested. Many were left worst off then they were before the project. To complicate not having the much needed water many depleted their savings.

The years of experience in the art of conserving water and applying it to only the best land made Posper, for many, a most beautiful spot in which to live. The neighboring villagers who tilled their thirsty land, spoke of it as "The Garden of Eden."

Once a year people would gather from neighboring villages to celebrate the bounteous harvest and enjoy themselves within the refreshing sight of fruit, berries and vegetables of seemingly endless varieties. Then with lagging hope, return to the disappointment of their meager farms to experience the poverty brought on by lack of water and drought.

One day the news was heralded abroad, a geologist by the name of
Harris had discovered that a dam could be built in Rollins Canyon. The
news soon spread that by storing the flood waters from the valleys above,
there would be sufficient water for many of the villages below, to quench
the thirst of their fertile soil.

It became the proverbial custom to delve into it's future benefit to
the valley as a whole. Many attempts were made to interest wealthy men
who could financially aid such an enormous project to invest.
Unfortunately non could be found with sufficient confidence in the future
of such an enterprise, to invest their better secured wealth.

As time wore on the weary villagers banded together and appealed
to the state, with no avail. Then with that last final effort before despair,
they prepared a hearing on the question before the Senate. To receive no
answer, until with unexpected suddenness it came forth,
"The Appropriation for the dam was passed."

When each villager heard the story, they would solemnly pause for
the moment to reflect. Then with renewed energy and purpose, they would
take up the popular stride of preparing to share in the great undertaking,
and spread the news.

Such were the conditions as Allen hurried towards Helen's home
before daylight.

The cool, refreshing breeze of the morning, playfully nodded the
tips of trees and plants alike as it warned of the oncoming day. Slowly the
dark shadows of the mountains began to change to the soft blanket of
shaded light, through which peeped the tips of the uppermost trees. Here
and there was a glistening star that still refused to hide it's face before it's
silently on-creeping foe. Many tints of color tinged the eastern horizon to
spread their soft shades into the retreating shadow.

The two decided to walk from Helen's home to the dam site to
meet her father later that day.

In the mist of this spender two struggling figures climbed, each
seeming to have it's own problem of ascent, moving from point to point
near the top of the threatening crags. Both moving with a heroic effort to
place themselves, where the view of the world seemed supreme. As the
sun slowly rose above them the browns, reds and yellows changed to a
living gold as the wonders of earth and sky flashed before their eyes.

"My wasn't that uniquely beautiful?"

"It's spender nearly blinded me. It was worth all that effort and more, to again see this wonderful sight."

Allen still a little winded replied, "Yes, this is a beautiful sunrise. I
didn't come all the way up this mountain just for that. There are so many
things we can see from here. The ridge we are sitting on, for instance,
look, it twists and winds about as far as the eye can see into those distant
mountains. Now it is getting light enough to see better, I want you to look
at that little peak sticking up way over south east of here. You see it looks
like one disk on tip of another. Each one a little smaller around and thicker
through than it's brother, until on top it appears as only a round button.
Follow the ridge as it twists and squirms toward us, notice it's beginning
to get larger and more ugly. It seems to be writhing from place to place
like a giant eel. It's slime gleams as the smooth round back moves up
close to us. Now look, it's gaping mouth and threatening fangs are
swallowing the very rock we're on.

Wait a minute you silly, gosh, I thought you were going to jump."

She regained her balance and exclaimed, "Whew, I was scared. I
guess I was dizzy from standing here too long. Let's sit down while I get
over this fright. Say Allen, you didn't need to be so darn mean getting
even with me that way."

They settled back comfortably against a rock while Helen leisurely
told of her many trips to this same spot. Each time to add new adventures
and beauty with the changing seasons of the year.

She then thoughtfully looked on her companion and said, "Allen, I
can see a lot of changes in you lately.

What is it that is worrying you?

Has something gone wrong?"

He took a moment to scrutinize her face, wondering what it was
she wanted to find out, he cautiously replied, "You see, things are not like
they used to be. I don't know just what it is---I used to enjoy playing ball
at this time of year, but lately there are too many questions I am trying to
find answers to many questions. One is geology, I can't say I know much
about it, just the little your father has taught me in his spare time."

Helen recalled his telling her the story of the prehistoric ocean
with it's tiny animals and vegetable life that were the first to take
possession of the sea. Over time these would change from one specie to
another, thus developing into a multitude and many varieties in the ocean
vastness.

The Helen admonished, "Come out of that mood, Mr. Man, and
listen to me for a minute. Do you remember telling me how father's earlier

teachings impressed you?

Why, you could tell me nearly every important step in the development of vegetable and animal life of the early periods, when the ocean contained all the living things of this earth. You remember the soft jelly-like fishes we now call the eel?

They didn't have a backbone then, but finally formed one as the many generations came and went. This fellow could move through the water faster than any animal up to his time.

From this type developed the fishes up to the giant whales we catch for oil today. You explained how the backbone developed first in the fishes, then came out on the land in the form of huge monsters.

These further developed and were divided into the thousands of species we find buried in the earth, and those we have today.

Even the human seems linked in this chain of changing life. Now, don't tell me you can't understand geology, when you know the changes of life that are written in the massive leaves of our prehistoric book; "The Earth's Crust". Very few ever become conscious of this books existence, and fewer open the leaves to get the history which it contains that is all past animal and vegetable life of this earth."

"Yes, Helen, I remember, but it seems that it ought to be more complicated than just what I know and I guess it is. The key to the record is covered up by technical terms and lack of information on how they lived.

How is their struggle in the past compared with our struggle for existence today?

Remember the comparison your father made between the species of the past and today's society?"

Helen looked up with a pondering look, "No, I don't recall any comparison. I guess it's one thing I never heard, or forgotten about. Go on, tell me about it."

Allen thought a moment to recall the story clearly, then continued, "Once upon a time, there was a peaceful part of the ocean where great numbers of little fishes lived gliding about from place to place, visiting each other, happy that the world contained so much for them of both pleasures and food.

Then one morning a great shadow appeared, which tapered off towards to ocean floor. The little fishes gathered in groups of thousands to speculate as to the meaning of this. Some believed it a good omen, others thought it was amusing, while others worried and warned that some great trouble was at hand. In the past their sages told them of times in the past when a great monster had depleted their numbers.

A word of warning was passed among them, when a great riffle began on the surface, as the shadow began to move. Fear gripped the little fellows as a huge cavern seemed to be coming their way, into which great numbers of their kind were disappearing. The great gap closed as it moved by, to bring into sight, the coarse, cruel body of a giant fish of their own kind. It raised near the surface and rested leaving the little fishes gripped with fear.

Many sorrowed for the loss of friends and relatives, while others again warned of the approaching disaster. The great fish repeated his decent to feed, until finally the multitude of little fishes were forced to believe in their peril and prepared themselves to meet their foe.

By now the monstrous fish had grown so accustomed to returning and gobbling-up his fill of the little fellows, that he was completely taken by surprise when he came swooping down to repeat his act of feeding, only to discover his mistake too late to change his course.

These little fellows had organized into an almost solid body. So, as he came charging in they met him in a mass, filling his mouth and throat, smothering and choking him to death. This act of defiance cost the lives of a number of little fishes, but their danger from this monster was over at last."

Allen thought a moment. "Yeah," he chuckled, "Then your father said, 'Young man, if ever you see someone trying to pauperize or enslave the people by making false promises, to take away the means of their livelihood, appose such an attempt and join those down trodden people, help them organize in a mass to appose their ruthless oppressors.

They may lose a few of their number but will win their freedom in the end.'"

Then pointing toward the canyon he continued, "I nearly got my mind off the story watching those big trucks come out of the narrows. There are three of them already. Gosh, look at their loads. I bet it's equipment for the dam."

Helen followed the direction of his finger and with amazement exclaimed, "Sure enough, they sure didn't wast any time getting on-the-job."

Each excitedly speculated as to the contents of the big trucks, while the trucks with their motors moaning climbed the long steep grade to the flat of the upper valley floor.

"Gosh, they are sure arriving early this morning. It reminds me of a few years ago when a circus came to town. All of us young fellows made special arrangements to be up early and watch them unload. Such a thrill we would get when we watched them feed the animals, they would fight and quarrel over their breakfast. That reminds me, we didn't bring a lunch with us. What time was it your father said he would come along and get us?"

Helen without turning her head answered, "About noon, but that is a long time yet."

Allen wondered what had drawn her attention so attentively, so he asked, "What are you watching so closely off towards the well?

It can't be your father, for you said he wouldn't be coming until noon. Say, is that someone coming along the trail?"

Helen immediately replied, "I've been watching him coming for about five minutes, I just thought it was someone hunting. He is following the trail that leads right up here."

Allen noticed the gait of the oncoming man and replied, "Well, it will be a long time at that gait before he gets here, so I guess we might as well hold our curiosity in check and watch the trucks unload.

Look, Helen, here comes another one, it's full of men. Surely, they're not going to start the whole project today."

They both intently watched the new truck as it climbed the grade to finally come to a stop with the other three trucks. Out of the truck climbed many men that seemed ready to get to work.

Helen began counting the men, when she finished she replied, "I believe, those are tents stacked on the first three trucks, so they must be going to build a tent city. There were twenty men in that last truck. That many men ought to be able to put up a lot of tents."

It was not very long until she proved to be right, for they separated into groups, each with a boss that directed them to unload the big trucks. They would unload a few tents and then the trucks would pull up a little to repeat the process until all three were unloaded.

The drivers called a parting word or two as they left on their journey back down the canyon.

The workmen returned the farewell then responded to the snappy voices of the bosses as they ordered each group to their various tasks. Each workman would procure a certain part, then methodically put it in place. There was hardly a moment of wasted effort as the framework rose, to finally be covered with a not too clean canvas to complete the tent.

Helen and Allen had become so absorbed in the building of the first tent, that the slow plodding figure climbing the mountain had been forgotten.

He would move up the hill a ways to find a comfortable place to sit and gain back his wind, then wipe the rivulets of perspiration from his face, then rise to begin again the long climb to the summit. Longingly he would peer though each grove of trees to the ridge beyond, hoping it would be the last. Then climbing to it's top he would see another beyond.

At last the thought stuck him, that when he reached the next ridge he would follow it up to the main ridge of the mountain, and ease his labor by not having to descend into the next hollow then up to the next rise. This helped him to move along faster for the paths were clear along the tops of the ridges, soon he was following the main ridge towards the highest point which was his goal.

Helen was first to notice that something had happened to the man who had been plotting towards them, nudging Allen she queried, "I wonder where that fellow went."

Allen looked in that direction for a few moments and replied, "I suppose he got tired and turned down one of the hollows. We'll see him come out down below later. Say, what do you think of that?"

He pointed back towards the tents and continued, "They finished ten of them and I believe I can hear more trucks coming up the canyon. Look, there is a car coming up the grade now. Say, it looks familiar, let's see."

Helen had been scanning the mountain to find their expected visitor, but hearing Allen mention a car, and particularly one he recognized, she turned quickly to see. With a sharp chilling voice remarked, "It's Royal Brinkly's car. I guess we'll see plenty of him from now on. It will take awhile to complete the dam."

Helen with a flushed face plucked at his arm to more surely draw his attention and pleaded, "Allen please don't renew the quarrel with him. Let the past be forgotten for I have a feeling that he will be waiting for revenge at the least excuse to try to even the score by fare means or foul."

Then with a pleading expression on her face continued, "So be very careful won't you."

Allen feeling her change of mood at the appearance of Royal's car sensed her feelings of responsibility for their being enemies replied, "Come now, don't get serious and worry about something that may never happen.

Do you remember scolding me for being in a doubting mood like that?

I don't think we have to worry for I believe either one of use can handle him at his worst. Say, how did we ever forget that lunch?"

Helen's face expressed an accusing smile as she spoke, "Do you remember mother handing it to you and saying, 'Now, Allen, I'll put this in your charge and I know it will be eaten.' but I guess it will taste as good when we reach the car as it would now. Nearly all my lunches receive the same treatment that I was supposed to take with me."

Allen reflected a moment, thinking of an answer and not being able to change the subject, when he heard a musical voice call out, "Is your name Miss Harris?"

They both jumped to their feet and turned to see outlined against the sky just above them a figure of abject poverty whose shoes had been badly used and many sizes too large, the trousers with many patches and badly worn. Showing above this, a large checkered flannel shirt drew their attention where the collar met the smiling face and rolling eyes of a middle aged man.

Chapter X

A New Character

"Now just a minute, folks. I didn't mean to frighten' yo' all, not a bit of it, but if you are Miss Harris." Addressing Helen, "I have your lunch."

She immediately recognized the large lunch pail which her mother frequently sent on such occasions. Seeing the intruder was beginning to be a bit frightened replied, "Yes, my name's Miss Harris and I am sure that is my lunch pail. How did you come in possession of it?"

With a crest fallen attitude he continued, "Well folks, that is long story, and seeing how you are kinda upset I better make it short. Yesterday I got kicked off a drag just over the hill yon way, it's the main line of the railroad Well, I had found out for sure where that dam is going to be. So I said to myself, 'Mighty lucky, I didn't get the boot back in the desert.' Well, so I picked myself up and said, 'doggone it, the railroad wasn't like this before. Leaving a fellow way out here alone with no rations, poor clothes, with no place to sleep, accept on the cold rough ground. Then I started on my way. Now children, I asks you, have you ever been hungry?"

Allen quickly invited, "Come on down here with us and don't forget to bring that lunch, for if you have ever been hungrier than I am right now it's when you were closer than I am to that lunch and knew you'd have a harder time getting it."

This gave him new courage, he gathered up the lunch and climbed off the rock and down to where they were standing. He took off his hat as if in respect and apologized, "Now don't let me disturb you all because I had better get on my way."

He handed the lunch to Allen then he turned to go, but Allen spoke firmly. "You'll do nothing of the kind. Come sit right down her and finish telling us the rest of your trip and how you got this lunch. We'll investigate what's in the pail for I think there will be plenty for all three of us."

Helen took the pail and began to place part of it on a rock so as to make it handy, for there was a variety fit for a real lunch.

Once they had seated themselves comfortably their visitor began, "Well, folks that sure was a long pull over the hill.

It was almost night when I spied a camp. Say, I just sprung up all new again and hurried right down there, The boss and his wife fixed me right up with eats, and asked me to stop and rest for a time, then asked me if I wanted to sleep in the tool house.

I sat down and pretty soon an argument started. Some of the folks in camp were commenting on how that "New Deal" (government programs of the 1930's) w as going from bad to worst and had swindled most everybody loose from their land and their jobs and that New Eagle (President Franklin D Roosevelt) i s flying so high he can't see the real trouble. Well sir, both of them buzzards has caused grief enough to fill the world with woe. With misery enough promised for the future to keep us in eternal torment for ever. Well folks, I must have been awful tired, for I don't remember going to bed but I woke up this morning before daylight to hear that inviting verse, 'Come an get it' and then I met your papa. He asked me which way I was going and I told him the whole story.

Well sir, he told me I could come right up here and see the whole show and if I was coming this way to bring your lunch to you for he thought I'd find you here, and if I didn't to keep it.

Well sir, I lost the trail and say, it got tough going. So I took to the ridge. I says to myself 'I'll take the highest point then I'd be sure to find you. And here I am. I don't see why the minute I go broke and out of a job my appetite almost gets me down."

He paused to relish the other half of his sandwich then continued, "Rich folks have the rations while poor folks have the appetite. I suppose they will fix that someday, by taking the poor man's stomach away from him."

Helen passed the lunch pail toward him again, he raised a hand in protest, "No, miss, I've eaten enough at the camp to last for some time. But woe is me is I don't get that job and make some money."

Allen enjoyed hearing him moan about his troubles and queried, "What would you do with money?"

"Me sir?

Well, every time I think of it I mighty near pass-out, for what I crave is action. I would play in with wine, women and the dice for company. But if I ain't lost the remembering part of my mind, Lady Luck has played me false and every one of us workers is in the same boat. There ain't no future for us while the big boy plays all hog or none, and with me it's been mostly none. Why, When I left the east the big boy was plumb running wild, because the workers were marching in the street and showing the trouble of the world. I was ambling along in one of them demonstrations when I got in a ruckus with the police folks, and they blamed a lot of bruised faces on me. So, the first chance I get I said, 'feet get a running and here I am."

Helen's pleasant voice trembled a little with laughter as she queried, "What kind of work do you usually do?"

"Well miss, I handle the wrong end of hard work. I take the place of the machine. Usually they have me mucking on the business end of a scoop or something and sometimes they let me rest while I'm wrestling things from one place to another. Lordy, I'll shore be glad when all we have to do is press a button and pull a lever while the steel eats up our work.

Well, I guess there's a lot of work to do first before that time comes."

Then he hauled in his gangling legs and drew his coat closer about him as if in habit of being chilly remarked, "Well, folks the main thing I better do right now is rear upon my own hind legs and pull the ring on my parachute and ooze down from this mountain."

He rose to his feet as he continued, "Them sandwiches sure tasted noble, well, folks, I'll be seeing you again if I get a job."

Then as if in the habit of talking to himself he began, "Feet get going before I lose my strength, your picnic is over."

Allen and Helen felt that they had been well entertained by one who seemed to understand the working class problem. They called a friendly farewell as the new acquaintance carefully shifted from one rock to another down the hill.

Allen noticed the occasional limp that brought up the state of his shoes, "Helen, did you notice his feet while he was eating here with us?

The soles were almost gone. His bare feet showed through in a place or two."

She had been watching him also as he limped and occasionally sat down to pick rocks and slivers from his feet. "The poor fellow. I surely feel sorry for a human who has to buck the world with all the odds against him. I surely hope he gets a job on the dam. If he hurries he can see Mr. Brinkly now and won't have to go downtown first."

They turned to watch the growing tent city and tried to formulate an idea of the number of people that would be there once the construction of the dam is in full swing. Not able to compare it to anything they had ever seen, they began to count the tents. Once they finished counting they discovered there were now twenty-five.

A low droning sound became audible off to the south of them that was now continually increasing in volume. It finally appeared with its body flashing in the sunlight above them. They could now see it against the blue sky circling several times just above the dam site. This caused them to speculate before they discovered a plausible reason for the planes peculiar antics.

It first nosed downward procuring an altitude below them giving each a sudden thrill as it appeared from their high position to be diving straight into the ground. Then it gracefully leveled off to make more short circles over the camp.

Helen saw someone leaning over the side and exclaimed, "I thought sure there was something wrong with the plane, but now I see what they are doing, they are taking pictures."

Allen gazed for some moments at the circling plane before he answered, "Yes, didn't they time their arrival accurate?

The men must have completed all of the tents, for they just stepped out as if they were settled in to see what all the commotion was. I hear the trucks coming again. If so, they ought to soon be in sight."

The people in the plan seemed to have finished taking pictures and soared away out of sight. With the distraction of the plan gone the men seemed to be free to roam from one place to another until the trucks arrived. Now the trucks could be plainly heard as the motors struggled to pull them up the steep grade.

Helen jumped to her feet and peered closely at the rocks below, this caused Allen to exclaim, "What Happened?"

There were several breathless seconds before she answered, "Our visitor has disappeared. I saw him last just on top of that ledge."

She pointed towards a jagged ledge that jutted out making a sheer drop of nearly fifty feet.

"He just slid out of sight between those two points.

Do you think we aught to make sure he is alright?"

Allen stood watching just below the ledge for any movement hoping he would again appear, when Helen exclaimed, "There he is, way down below where he was following the foot of those ledges.

I wonder how he got there?

I want to see how he got down there when we go to meet father."

Allen looked up at the sun to judge it's position and remarked, "I believe it's ten o'clock. It's about two hours before we need to meet your father. Let's walk around awhile."

Arm in arm they picked their way across the rocks to a flower strewn meadow bordered by small pine and willows.

"This is a sure place to find a deer along the top of this ridge. I've seen them several times when I've been here camping with the boy scouts.

Shall we take a little hike along it and see if we can see one?"

They moved along the ridge and as they were crawling through a thick clump of underbrush they were stopped by that prickly Dennison of the forest, the porcupine. This clever fellow sat upon his hind legs with his spiked back and tail always pointed towards them. He peered around his side with only one eye to be sure his tail was in perfect position as he waited.

"Say, he's a smart rascal. He thinks he has us at a disadvantage, but watch."

Allen picked up a good stiff stick and touched his tail with it. A quick slap of the tail threw the stick to one side leaving several quills sticking in it, but the porcupine stayed on the trail in front of them. Allen tried it again, the stick received the same treatment. He then pulled the stick back and showed it to Helen.

"You see, that's the way he fixes a dog when one tries to bother him. Those quills just keep working into the victim until they finally come out on the other side of him, if they are not pulled out, I suppose you already knew that."

She quickly denied, "No, I didn't know the quills had means whereby they could crawl."

Allen then pulled a quill out of the stick and explained, "There are small notches all the way up from the point. Each notch is formed like a barb on a fishhook. It will go in, but then catches a firm hold when you try to draw it out. So, each time it is touched or the victim moves it's point goes in deeper. Well, that's about all we want to bother with him, now watch."

Allen then gave him a good dig with the stick which made him grunt similar to a pig. Now with a disgusted look he guardedly waddled out of their way letting them continue on their way.

When they came out on the opposite side of the thicket Allen philosophized, "Some people are just like that porcupine they become stubborn because they have had their own way too long. They think this earth just turns for them and them alone. They've forgotten to consider the millions around them that are being oppressed because of their slowness in understanding others situations. The comfortable need to help gather the oppressed class and change the world and make it fit to live in."

He looked toward Helen and smiled as he continued, "Now, don't blame that saying on me. I never thought it out like that, but I just remember the professor saying it that way. I tried to study it out and I'm in sympathy with every part of it that I understand."

Helen had almost become dumbfounded hearing expressions from him like this, so she queried, "The professor must have been giving you some heart to heart talks the last couple of days."

"No, but I listened to your father and him discus a few of the economic questions the other night, but they finally got too deep for me to even follow what they were talking about, so I just had to leave them to it and amuse myself some other way. We had better get along faster, we'll have to hurry if we expect to see a deer today."

Happily they moved from one point to another, anticipating each moment to frighten a beautiful specimen of wild life from it's refuge. Their spirits began to lag after they had tramped over the rough ridges for half an hour.

Then Helen saw a doe and fawn and become so excited she ran up the ridge to watch it bounce out of sight in the timber below. She didn't notice Allen running in the other direction. She became aware he was no longer with her and immediately looked around to see where he went but to no avail, he seemed to have evaporated. A nervousness overcame her as she climbed to the top of the ridge but she couldn't see a soul.

Moments seemed like hours as fear for his safety brought lines of worry to her face. Then her thoughts formed into words, "What could have happened to him?"

Patiently she watched as the moments dragged on. Finally a thought struck her and with hurried steps she followed her tracks to the place they parted to find his footprints. They went down in the opposite direction.

The many questions that entered her mind only made a jumble in her mind. Each foot seemed to weigh a ton as she labored along. The footprints led to the ledge where they were lost on the smooth surface of the rock. She could feel herself going weak so with little else to do she sat down.

In a last effort to control her feelings she burst forth in a pleading call, "Allen."

"Is that you Helen, come give me a lift, I can hardly make it alone."

Like winding up a run down clock, she received new vigor from his words. Alert to the danger she neared the edge of the ledge and peered down to see Allen desperately clinging to an out-jutting rock on the face of the cliff.

Chapter XI

Just A Slip

A new interest was developing at the little camp which nestled snugly at the valley floor. The heavy drill with its rhythmic churning was slowly but surly biting its labored way deeper towards the oil bearing sands. It had been a disappointing task to patiently, day after day, month after month, gradually play out the line to feel the bit surge to greater depths. At times sticking causing a heavy drag on the drill, It had to be jerked free to relieve the tension on the throbbing machinery. Once the bit was free the motor would run smother as it reamed the hole, making it now safe to proceed.

The driller, a quiet patient man, could not see his important task, yet as he calmly stood with his hand to the line, he appeared to be one with the rhythmic motion of his vibrating machines.

This day it was not only the driller who patiently waited the return of the bit to the surface, for Helen's father had carefully examined the core samples. Each core he laid in order to see the subtle changes from one to the next. With surprise and quickened enthusiasm, he examined the sump where he discovered a rainbow of many shapes and hues glistening in the sunlight. This brought out the excitement that always drove the old prospector within. The rainbow indicated the "Black Gold" that he had hoped would relieve his financial tension.

He tried to instill within the stockholders of the company the hope that was built on a standing offer. His heart raced as he thought of the letter he had received, he remembered the letter's wording even now:

"Be it understood between this company and yourself, as president of your company, that at any time there is sufficient showing of oil, or gas, or both to warrant the dome's further investigation from a commercial standpoint please notify us and we will act immediately to make our offer a substantial one."

He thought of that letter each time he watched the sump for evidence of enough oil to warrant an investigation.

Now the long delayed feelings of relief was beginning to show on him. He was becoming overcome with a desire to hurry the process of time, to move the machinery at a faster gait, but everything seemed to lag, to jar his patience. Most of all he was becoming annoyed at the calm listening attitude of the driller.

Every moment seemed to lengthen to an unending agony as he waited tensely as the time passed while the driller brought the stem on it's long journey to the surface. Five minutes would pass with more of his show of impatience, then ten and fifteen to bring the long steel stem up the shaft. This time it came out shining like a pencil with changing colors that dazzled the eyes with its gleam in a shaft of sunlight. Dripping from it's end was the oily ooze that formed a pool on the drill room floor.

The sight of it brought thrills that nearly carried him on to ecstasy. Now with sudden determination and self control he mastered his feelings so he could calmly stride toward the gleaming stem to dig a sample from its bit. He took a small portion in his hand and added it to the others in his collection.

He had forgotten the time of day until like an explosion came those cheering words "Come and get it" from the smiling face of the driller's wife.

This meal he enjoyed more than any he had eaten in a long time.

He would be glad when the transactions were over and he would be relieved of this business burden. The depression times had made nearly all the stockholders either unwilling or unable to carry on much farther. Money had been hard to raise, making the responsibility on him even greater, to the point the stress was tiring him out. With this new development at the well he needed to hurry home and call a meeting of the stockholders to report the progress and decide their future.

Now with the immediate concerns settled, he departed to meet Helen and Allen at the dam site. As he approached the site he noticed a great many tents with figures of many men sprinkled among them. Some were unloading heavy equipment off of great trucks. The singsong sound of cursing and swearing men was very audible when he stopped, but nowhere could he see the object of his search.

He left his car and wandered from one place to another, interested in the suddenness that this tent city had come together.

At this moment he was investigating the new town Helen was helping Allen get to the top of the ledge with his spotted burden.

She inquired in earnest, "Did you get hurt?"

He responded with a definite,

"No"

She put her arms around his neck and with joy kissed him.

"Now that is no fair picking on me when my hands are full. Here take this fawn and I'll see what I can do about it."

She backed away and replied, "That will do for now. I guess a girl has a right to release her feelings after a scare like that, I really didn't know what had become of you."

She then took special notice of the squirming form in his arms and continued, "Isn't that the cutest thing?

Its nearly as spotted as a leopard, and look at those round eyes. I believe they can see all around themselves at once. Its legs are so long and thin, I don't see how they keep from breaking off or bending when they run. Let's sit down here for awhile and you can tell me how it happened."

He placed the fawn between them and with a hearty laugh began, "I don't believe it was us that frightened the deer. Anyway this fawn and its mother went one way and the big buck the other. Well, somehow just as they were going along the top of the cliff, the fawn slipped and struck its mother's leg bowling it over. It tried to regain its feet but too late, it slid over the edge of the cliff. I rushed over to see it struggling about ten feet below.

It had wedged between two jutting rocks. I had to hurry for it was beginning to get loose, if it had, it would have fallen and been flat as a pancake down below. Well, I made it in time only to find I had to have both hands to climb back up. Once I had it in my arms the darn thing started kicking and for several moments I wished I had left it alone."

She looked up with a scolding expression, "Why, Allen, you know you don't mean that. The poor little thing, it enjoys to live just as much as we do. I'll tell you what, let's take it with us, I heard the driller say he would like one for a pet."

Allen did not have time to answer, for suddenly the fawn sprang to its feet nearly escaping the hand which closed around its leg. he scolded, "Now, it's in your care, if you hadn't caught it again, our worries would have been over."

Helen drew it back to her lap scolding all the while. The fawn sensing something out of the ordinary, settled passively into a round ball with only the long ears to betray it's presence.

Allen moved closer and put his arm around Helen's waist and smilingly remarked, "It's your turn to be the one armed sport. Don't you let go of that fawn."

Throwing her head back she accepted his lips in a prolonged and tantalizing caress.

Blushing she regained her composure, while handing him the spotted prize she persuaded. "Now, my ardent lover, you take this fawn and let's be going for I believe father will be waiting for us."

He put the struggling prize over his shoulders. They then started on the return journey for the lunch pail as Allen remarked, "Darn it, I wish we had that pail with us now. We could save some hard climbing and quite a little distance by cutting down around the ridge."

"Oh, no, you don't, go around and miss that ledge where our friend disappeared to come out fifty or a hundred feet below. I'd like to see how that was done and maybe try it myself. Of course, one of us may have to go around with the deer, but we can draw lots to see who does that."

Jogging along at an easy gait the lunch pail soon appeared in sight.

"Allen, you cut across to the ledge and I'll get the bucket."

She hurried ahead at a snappy trot so that she soon joined him. Together they came up to view the drop off where the middle aged man disappeared. With much awe and apprehension they both stood staring at the narrow trail, nearly straight down and curving towards the cliff so it could not be seen from above or below, until one was right up close.

"Well, wouldn't that get you. I've seen this cliff many times before but this is the first time I ever saw that trail. Come on I'll go first."

Helen glanced down the trail where she could see the footprints of their previous visitor. With reassurance she replied, "All right, now do be careful the weight of the fawn may make it dangerous going."

Carefully he stepped in the tracks that were made ahead of him, followed closely by Helen. Every careful step increased the danger of the steep decent. Suddenly the shale under their feet quivered, Helen, being the most nervous, gave a started cry of alarm as she reached down and grabbed Allen's out-flung arm.

A sickening feeling gripped their stomachs as they shot violently along the cliff that tore there clothes, bruised their legs, arms and bodies. A thunderous roar filled their ears as the rocks and dust of the mountain spun around them as they fell. Their eyes were soon pounded shut, as rocks and dirt filled their noses and throats. Fear paralyzed their senses as they slipped into the black void of unconsciousness.

He dodged and countered those bony fingers of death that seemed to reach for him. He struck out to repel those ghastly unblinking eyes that gleamed from that leering face. Relentless and cruel was its onslaught, until, with one final effort Allen affected his escape from death, to climb back to the light.

Now that the battle with death was behind him he began to see a small red glow, then he cleared the shadow from his eyes so he could feel the full glare of day on his face. The sun's heat was warm and caressing as it brought him back his senses. He then rubbed the dirt from his eyes so he could see where he landed.

He could now feel something heavy on his chest, he tried to move it to relieve his aching lungs. He felt a sudden shock back to consciousness when his hand touched the smooth warm flesh of Helen's body. In this dizzy whirl of events she had landed across his chest and face.

The realization came to him that it was her body that he thought was death trying to suffocate him. He gathered up his strength so he could sit up and see her. To his dismay Helen's face was white and there was not even a quiver in the muscles of her sweet face.

Her clothes were ripped but in spite of the fall she had few scratches and seemed to have no broken bones. His deep concern subsided and his hope returned when he saw the slow rise and fall of her chest and the color came back to her face.

A few minutes passed when her eyes slowly opened and stared blankly up at him, her lips parted to speak then paused on the first syllable. Her eyes again closed and an expression of peace came over her face.

Patiently he waited, hoping for the best but expecting the end before her breathing became more frequent and a quiver ran through her body. Her eyelids twitched as a signal she was alright, then they slowly opened to look around. The surroundings seemed to come into focus dimly for a few moments passed before she spoke, "My I am glade you are alright, I feel so tired and weak. Just let me rest this way for a while, I believe I'll be alright soon."

With a catch in his throat he smoothed the wavy locks of hair from her brow, receiving in return an appreciative glance accompanied by a slight smile. Little did she realize at this moment her plight. The plain print dress she had been wearing was now rent to shreds, exposing the ugly bruises on her trim and well formed limbs.

A slight tinge of color crept to his face as he carefully drew the ruined dress together to cover her near nude condition. He then queried, "How are you feeling now?"

"Better, help me sit up, I believe you need to move your legs to see if they are hurt."

There were a few moments of giddiness before he could attempt to sit up.

Seeing his worried face she asked, "Whats wrong? Are they broke?"

Allen tried to suppress the anguish he felt when he answered, "No, I think not, they feel paralyzed as far as moving them is concerned. Of all the aggravating conditions there's a tickling sensation running up and down them which tends to prickle like pins and needles. The worst of it is, I can't move them, or, I believe, I could get some relief if I could kick them together."

Helen remembering that feeling of pins and needles suggested, "Shall I rub them for you or are they bruised too badly?"

He gritted his teeth together and nodded accent while she, feeling many sharp pains, pluckily raised to her knees and began a brisk rubbing of his legs from ankle to thigh.

"Gee, they are sure coming to life, thank you." all of sudden a thought struck him that there was one of their number missing, "Helen, have you seen the deer?

I don't remember a thing about where it went after you took hold of me. Too many things happened at once to worry about such a small trifle as just one deer."

He showed as much pain as he could muster as he got up to hide his embarrassment, he then met her sympathetic gaze as she gave him a playful scolding, "If any of us three are dears it's you, for without you for a landing spot, I believe, I would have been killed." then with wonder she continued, "You must have held me quite awhile before I came too?"

Helen looked around wondering what had happened to their four legged friend, when what was apparently a small leaf turned over to lay there a second and then turned back again. Nudging Allen she pointed to a pile of rubbish and exclaimed, "Doesn't his color match the background perfect?

If he hadn't blinked an eye I don't believe we would have found him without putting out some real effort."

Helen stood in suspense while Allen carefully crept nearer to the fawn. With every step they expected it to jump to it's feet and scamper away. The only sign of life was the big staring eyes looking up at him. Certain it would make a final effort to escape he quickly took hold of it's neck, not one quiver of resistance met his move.

Allen called back to Helen, "Well, he must be hurt, come here and let's see what's the mater."

A short examination revealed he was only slightly hurt on his back, with a little coaxing and some effort on its part the deer could stand alone. Once again they loaded it on Allen's shoulder then continued on their careful decent down the mountain slope.

Seeing Helen's dismay Allen queried, "You can have whats left of my shirt if you can use it."

With great relief Helen answered, "I surely would appreciate it. I don't believe it's me they will be watching, for our prize will draw a lot of attention, I think it wouldn't be long until I would too.

We will soon come to a favorable place at the foot of the next ridge where it flattens out, they shouldn't be able to see us from below so you can take it off for me there."

Once there he gave her his shirt, with a few well placed rents the shirt was converted to an apron, not with much merit but sufficiently appropriate to discourage rude remarks or prying eyes.

Now that she felt more confident she encouraged him to use more speed in their decent, so it took them only a few minutes to get to the car.

When Helen saw her father coming toward them she could see that he had grown impatient while waiting for them, She greeted him with a big smile, "Come now, father, we have more bad news for you."

He seemed to already understand, as he began, "Yes, I saw the fawn.

What are you going to do with it?

Look at you two.

What the deuce happened?

Neither one of you have enough clothes left to flag a bread wagon."

Helen quickly changed the subject as she replied, "If you're in a hurry we had better be going back to the well and deliver our deer to the driller. He said he wanted one for a pet."

Her father stepped into the car as he replied, "Hmm----yes, I suppose he will be tickled to have a nuisance like like that around."

Helen resenting the upset reflected in his voice responded, "Father, you know it's lonesome up there without something to distract your mind from the steady thump and grown of machinery. I'll bet his wife will like it too."

Mr. Harris's disposition was soon calmed as he listened to the thrilling experiences of the morning and with the addition of the joy expressed by the driller and his wife over their new addition of the deer. He soon joined in the pleasant conversation that included the usual joking and laughing.

When they returned to the dam site they were surprised by a number of loaded trucks that blocked the narrow grade leading to the camp.

Patiently Mr. Harris leaned back in the seat and began, "As bad as I want to get home, all this has to happen, well, it only goes to show how blamed insignificant one or two humans are compared to the onward march of events.

Take for instance the oil well we're drilling up the valley. We are starting to get results so the government comes up with a big project to provide more work for men that results in one nice big dam that covers a beautiful prospect for an oil field with seventy-five feet of water.

My ambition is to get the natural resources of our world discovered and put into use for man's benefit, these things seem to get in the way of this ambition.

Of course, one has to live while doing his bit, lately it has been a question of rather to continue the well or just let it drop until some future time.

Over the last two years nearly all of the stock-holders have gone broke or badly bent, now I would like to see them get something out of their investment, that is, if it's possible."

Allen had been listening with keen interest, now he saw his chance to add his opinion, "yes, I think of all the life or energy it took to make that pool of oil, now they are going to cover it with water. When they finish that dam how can the oil be taken out? It seems to me that it would cost more to deliver it than it's worth."

"Yes, Allen you're right. If we don't sell the well to some big company before it's covered with water it means "finis" for our little company. That's why I am in such a hurry to get home. The well is thirty-eight hundred feet deep and the last hundred has been very encouraging.

This morning when we stopped the drill the sump bailing was covered with oil. I believe if the stock-holders see it the way I do, we can sell it to a prospective buyer I have in mind and at least retrieve part of the money we invested.

Of course that won't solve future problems, it just makes big business' bigger and wipes out their competitors. Then these big companies can wait and manipulate the making of laws to their advantage to make their money."

The last big truckload pulled by. Mr Harris could now turn his attention to the open road ahead, he released the brake to go in second gear down the steep grade.

Helen saw a man running up the road waving frantically, cautioned, "Father, he wants you to stop, there must be something in the way."

Chapter XII

Gruesome Humor

"Hey there, could you----why, hello Mr. Harris, how are you?

An if it ain't Miss Harris and Allen, well, well. You remember that job I spoke about when I left you, well, sir I got it. But Lordy, shaking his head to emphasize, "Such a job, I go to work and first thing, they bring me down here to help with the steam shovels. What do you think, I'm the luckiest man in the world, for don't you know, something went wrong with the apparatus and first thing I know I kinda feel or hear something and blows just like that." He threw his hands apart then rolled his eyes until the whites of them were most prominent.

"The big bucket just messed up things awful. Well, sir, I just went paralyzed, then when I turned about I see two men, that I was working with smashed up."

Helen's father now deeply interested inquired, "Are they hurt or are they dead?"

"That just it, they were hurt, but the bad luck he fixed them up, I am suppose to ask you if you can take the remains to town?"

His hurry to tell what had happened kept him so "out of puff" that he could be hardly understood, so Helen anxiously asked, "You mean they are dead then?"

"Yes, mam, that's it, they are dead as old Solomon himself, and if you don't believe, come on down and see for yourself, I feel lucky I didn't get it in the neck."

Helen's father preparing to move on replied, "Jump on, Sam, we'll go down and see, maybe we can take them along,"

It was a gruesome sight that met their eyes. Very few of the workers took notice of them as they drove up to get the bodies. The work continued as the men toiled with sweat while the big shovel ate big gulps of the hill, swinging to spew it out on the lower side of the road.

Once in place they got out of the car and walked toward the bodies. They were startled by a gruff voice that suddenly called out, "If I see any one of ya' slacken up whilst I'm away, I promise it will be the last of you on this job."

Helen edged over close to Sam and asked, "Does he talk to the men like that all the time?"

Sam look up at her with surprise and answered, "Oh yes, Miss, that is the way it is on all of these big jobs. They just get the last once of life that is in you and let the buzzards to the rest. Proven by all the accidents."

By this time the red faced man of authority came within earshot and stopped all conversation when he expounded, "The loafers, nary a one is any good, you can't get good men like you used to. Now look at these two." Pointing disgustedly at the dead men, "Neither one of them had life enough to step away from the bucket. Just stood there with mouths agape and let it drop right on them. Why, I never seen the likes. Just pure laziness that's what I call it. Now, Mister, if ya can take them down for me, I'll sure appreciate it, for every one of them are in pretty bad shape. It'd take some fixing up before they get cold or their identification will be impossible."

"No, I'll take the responsibility. I'll send a note." Stopping a moment to meditate he began again, "Sam here will do, I'll send it with him.

How about it Sam?"

Sam looked a little hesitant as he stammered, "Well-a-um, Sure, but Mr. Harris."

Holding up his hand for quiet Mr. Harris calmed him, "Now, Sam, that's alright. You just get up front with Helen and Allen, I'll ride with the dead men."

The foreman completed the note, read it aloud then handed it to Sam, "Now, Sam, give that note to the general foreman. He's at the depot, he'll take care of the rest. Now, Mr. Harris, I believe if you'll just drop them off at the depot with Sam, the foreman will fix it up with ya."

He called men that submissively came over with one at each end carried the unfortunates to the car and placed them inside. The still impatient geologist followed them and ordered, "Allen you drive, we'll have to go back a ways, about where we met Sam and take the road over the hill. It will be quicker than waiting here an hour while they finish this cut."

They were once again on their way, now with the cruel evidence of the working man's lot. Allen reflected, 'either the working man must be a slave to be driven to the end of his endurance for a mere pittance and then die.' 'or it is their destiny to be wiped out by the cruel mistakes of malignant or ignorant overseers?"

"What did you say Mr. Allen, were you talking to me?"

Allen did not realize his thoughts were being transmitted to words, since he did he asked Sam, "What do you think about it?"

"Well sir, if you ask me, it seems like the world is infested with poor bosses and hard work, every time I get a job it's the same thing. Far as I can see the working men need to get together and do something for himself. The rich man is organized against us poor folks to get everything we have. Even our lives."

Helen nudged Allen notifying him it was her turn, and asked, "What would you do about it?"

Rubbing his wrinkled brow as if perplexed he began, "Well, Missy, the rich man says, 'I build the dam and if it wasn't for my money there wouldn't be a dam.' So he sets himself out in the front and demands the power and the glory for ever and ever, amen. I claim there ain't no dam, no money and no rich man to smoke see-gars without first there is the hard working class to steal it from.

Now when I began sweating on these four-bit jobs, I tell the boys, 'Don't yo' all know that it's us poor folks that do all the work. Can't you see, the rich man hire the bosses to drive the life out of with hard work while he sits back and watches the money roll in. Don't yo' all want to eat better, wear better clothes and watch the machines to the hardest work?

If yo' all do, we better make us a union and organize all the poor people together and demand more wages. Then if the big boys don't like it we can strike and picket the job. Then his money stops coming in. Of course, we get in a ruckus once in awhile but we are going to win in the long run."

Helen continued to draw him out with, "How do you know all of this Sam?"

"Now, Missy, I suspect you know something about this yourself, I will tell you I been poor all my measly life. I have had to work or I just can't eat. I've been with the boys when they won more wages and when they didn't have no work, I have been with them when we stuck together and we win."

"Yes, Sam, I believe you're right, although I haven't been in a demonstration, I've heard and read quite a bit about them and come to think it takes solidarity of the workers and farmers to win any progress in our civilization."

Allen had traveled along at a good rate of speed so he soon pulled up to the station platform and reminded, "Sam, it is up to you. Where are you going to put these dead men?"

With a sudden start Sam responded, "Now, Mr. Allen, just a minute, I'll find the foreman and be right back."

Moving along with that ease of motion that denotes plenty of reserve strength, he soon returned with a tall nervous man with roving eyes that seemed to take in every detail around him.

He came up to the car and asked, "Sam says you have some men here for me. Am I right?"

Mr. Harris stepped out of the car and replied, "Yes, we have a couple. Where shall we put them?"

"Put them!! What do you mean?"
Sam began to sputter, "Yes, sir, I forgot, here is the note my foreman sent to you." He dug deep in his pockets in a moment pulled out a badly crumpled note and handed it to the foreman.

His quick roving eyes soon took-in the contents of the note and with no other questions ordered, "Unload them right here, I'll have the dead wagon come right up."

The first man was taken from the car, he was placed with his back on the platform giving them all a queer feeling, his muscles had stiffened in the sitting position. When they left him to get the other the first rolled over and fell to a lower platform.

Helen screamed a warning that was taken for fright, causing Sam's hair to stand on end then Sam just moved a way until the confusion settled down.

He then returned keeping his eyes on the corpses as he replied, "Now, Missy, don't you ever do that if you can help it. Because if there is anything that gets my jitters up, it's the rattle of dead mans bones or the blood curdling voice of the spirits."

The nervous foreman in a business like manner offered to pay for the service rendered, only to receive in reply. "No, that's alright, I'll be over to the dam once-in-a-while and there will be plenty of chance to get even with you then."

They then climbed into the car then all three called out at once, "Good-bye, Sam, we'll be seeing you again."

Once the car was moving toward home Helen's father asked, "Where are you two going? I have an important meeting to attend to. So I'll need to drop you off one place or another."

Helen quickly replied, "You had better take me home so I can get some decent clothes on. I think mother would like to see you anyway. You do remember her telling you she would have lunch ready about four o'clock. It's getting about that time."

A worried expression showed on her father's face as he exclaimed, "What else is going to happen to delay me? I've been ever since noon trying to get back to town so I could see some of the stock-holders. Now I guess I had just as well go home and call them on the phone first."

It was a ragged looking pair that Helen's mother saw step from the car and come running to the house causing many questions to fill her mind. Once she heard their footsteps on the porch she left the window to meet them.

"For heaven's sake, what has happened to you two?"

Helen began untying the makeshift apron as she replied, "Oh, we just had a slight accident, the mountain got tired of holding on to us and dropped loose about five tons of rocks and dirt with us among it."

As she threw the shirt carelessly to one side her explanation was suddenly checked by her mother's warning voice, "Good gracious, Helen, don't you know you are naked. Get right out of here quick and get some clothes on. For shame, to stand before a young man looking like that."

Helen turned and faced her mother and chided, "Mother, don't always be so afraid of anyone's nakedness affecting their moral character. Can't you understand, these are the days of nude camps and bathing resorts. You know, I am better clothed now than when I'm in a bathing suit."

Her mother looking sadly towards her and responded, "Yes, Helen, I'm sorry I spoke so harshly, we were raised different in my younger days. The exposure of one's person before the male sex before marriage was to condemn oneself, not only before God but before the whole community in which one lived. Calling for dire need of repentance."

Then speaking directly to Allen she continued, "You'll forgive me won't you? I didn't mean to insinuate but now I notice you are a bit exposed yourself. Helen, you go and get one of your father's shirts for Allen while he washes up."

The worried figure of her husband strode through the door to meet her cheery greetings, "Come now, Herbert, get yourself washed for I'll soon have lunch ready."

He walked up to her and gently patted her on the shoulder as he replied, "Honey, we have a mighty good showing at the well today. I'll need to get on the phone right away to see what the rest of the boys want to do about selling it. If we don't it's all over with for us. The water at the well will be at least seventy-five feet deep when the dam is full. We can hardly raise enough money now to keep our expenses on the well paid up."

He gazed out the window for a moment, then seemed to gain new inspirations so with a more cheerful note in his voice continued, "I'll call Wilson and have him talk to the rest of the boys while I eat."

As he passed through the door he reminded, "I'll be ready for that lunch in a minute."

It was a pleasing reunion as the four of them came from the different parts of the house to meet in the dinning room.

Helen's father controlled the situation as he began, "Well, the boys took me at my word when I spoke about it the other day and Wilson says they're ready to sell any time it can be done. So let's get busy at this lunch. When we're done I will be on my way to the telegraph station. What have the rest of you planned to do this evening?"

Helen's mother quickly spoke, "I have some folks coming from out of town tonight, Herbert, I'd like you to be home if you can."

Consenting to be there if his business did not indicate differently, her husband glanced at Helen as she replied, "Allen and I are going over to talk to the professor for awhile tonight. That is, if I can make it that far. Gosh, I'm surely stoved-up since that tumble in the rocks. How about you Allen? Didn't you get bruised too?"

He touched a sore spot or two as he replied, "I sure did, but they don't hurt much unless I touch them."

Once lunch was finished Helen's father left, leaving her and Allen helping with the dishes in preparation for the evening.

Once the house was tidied up her mother excused herself. Then like a pare of Siamese twins, they tripped arm in arm towards the gate to wait for her father's return.

When Helen's father pull up, he parked the car and called to them, "I suppose we have sold the well, the representatives of the buyer will be here tomorrow or the next day. Mr. Craig apologized for not being able to come himself."

Helen became excited at the mention of Mr. Craig and interrupted her father. "Is his initials B. A.?"

He nodded in the affirmative so she continued, "I'll bet that's the B. A. Craig the professor knows. Father do you remember me telling you about the baby from the train wreck? Well, that's his grandfather and if it is, judging from the letter he sent the babies mother, he's a dirty belly robber and a skinflint, so watch out when you're dealing with him for that's how he made his money in the past."

With keen interest they soon gleaned all the knowledge he had of this clever business man. With resolute purpose they walked along discussing the question; What ever happened to the little curly haired baby?

Helen soon became absorbed in her own thoughts as she let them carry her back to her and Allen's meeting just before the train-wreck, how it happened at an opportune time to bring them closer together in giving aid to the unfortunates then welding a friendship between them that she hoped would never be broken. She could feel a silent yearning within bringing to her that ancient urge of a home and family of her own, silently she weighed the balance: What chance had they for a home in these trying times with everything so unsettled. Half of the working men of the day were out of a job, either part time unemployed or forced to find the public charities to exist. No, better they be companions in the trials and pleasures of life as it comes than to follow that urge to rear children and enslave them to the selfish desires of a fiendish profit taking few.

Allen seeing something wrong inquired, "what are you so worried about? Trouble shows all over your face. Come on, a penny for your thoughts."

"No, Allen, I don't want to tell all my secrets."

"You don't? I'll tell you what I'll do. If you will tell me what you were thinking, I will tell you what I was thinking."

"Alright, you are on. Well, I was wondering what would happen to a little curly headed fellow if the rich grandpa had to assume its care. Especially if he had already had some excuse to slough this responsibility on to others, while he gloated over his wealth and refused the child's care. I am surely anxious to hear what the professor has to say about it. You remember, he said it was a long story and he would tell it some time when we were both there to listen. If the world didn't come to an end, tonight is the time we will both be there to hear the story of the rich man and his grandson."

Chapter XIII

Problems at School

A surprise greeted them when they returned to the cozy little cottage Allen always knew as home. The signs of life did not appear that normally made it the welcoming abode he had always enjoyed. No lights played their dazzling beams from the well curtained windows into the gathering dark. The hardwood door was closed, keeping within the families secrets of life so that their problems were barred from the world.

A puzzled expression crossed Allen's face.

Why all the darkness and quiet on such a warm and pleasant evening? Many such questions were coursing through his brain while he crossed the small porch to open the door.

He heard no one, he gently called, "Come on, Helen, let's see what is the matter here. It looks as though there isn't anyone home."

She was stooping to pick up a flower or two as she questioned, "What is your hurry? I'll be there in a minute."

He strode from one neatly prepared room to another just to be partially disappointed though greatly relieved at not finding something wrong.

When he walked back to the living room, he saw a happy, trim figure standing in the doorway, "Well, what do you think about it Helen? I don't see a soul around here, or any sign of a note telling where they went."

He sprang to the divan as though to shake off his disappointment then continued, "I suppose we just as well settle down and enjoy ourselves until they come home. I'll tell you what. We haven't an album but mother has a few pictures in her trunk. Let's get them out and take a look, I've only seen them a couple of times in my life."

This seemed to Helen to be a serious offense, going into his mother's trunk to get pictures which she didn't care to have in sight of prying eyes, so she questioned, "I don't believe I would get them if I were you. Your mother may feel embarrassed to know we have been through her trunk, it will surly look as if we have been snooping when they come home and find us looking through those pictures,"

His shoulders drooped in submission as he playfully came over to her and questioned, "It sure must be a touchy affair to bother a woman's things. Gosh, I haven't got a thing I'd be worried about if it was hung outside for the world to see,"

With a sudden outburst of feelings, she replied, "Yes, men have always demanded an 'out to the world' attitude, both in their thinking and doing of things. It is very different with women. We have been browbeaten into submission in everything they have thought or tried to do. We have to have places to hide our secrets where we could at times dig them out again to view our past lives with fear or pleasure. I'll tell you the day is coming when women will not be ashamed and neither will men, to meet the world of nature and subdue it to their comfort and pleasure with a common understanding of our thoughts and desires. You know as well as I do, it's just pure ignorance for one or the other to think they should know or do something the other can not."

"Now, dear young lady, if that was meant for me you'll have to wait a minute while I absorb a little of it at a time. It seems to me the whole trouble started when that old timer made the mistake, if I remember right, it was when he allowed someone to make him feel foolish, and become a laughing stock in the future, by plucking just one rib and starting it out to gain the world in competition to him. Seeing as how it happened that way, I guess the only thing to do about it is to take this rib along and see if it will become a man like the rest of us."

She caught him by the shoulders as she smilingly replied, "You would like to make monkey's out of us women, but I think there are many a she monkey that would be ashamed to claim the average run of men as their own."

Allen allowed himself to gaze into the deep mystery of her laughing eyes before he exclaimed, "Have it your way if you will. I'm sure glad I list among the majority so I don't come in for any of that special female attention. Say, I believe that is the picture I was thinking about."

He pointed to the table, the top picture in an opened box showed a handsome young man of about twenty with dark eyes and black wavy hair. He dominated the picture with an air of confidence and understanding.

Helen was first to make a comment as they viewed the picture from top to bottom, "That couldn't be the anyone but the professor, to think he's lived all these years among the fair sex and is still single. Well, hurry and turn that one over before I fall in love with it."

He complied with her request the next picture seemed to be a duplicate of the living Allen.

"Which is this? One of you or your father when he was young?"

He looked up with an assumed air of importance as he replied, "Now, you see, I was right when I told you I was one of the majority. This is me here,"

He put his thumbs up as if to put them in his vest, with a show of dignity he continued, "The picture is of my father and to prove further-" He paused to expose the next picture he continued, "That I am right, here is------"

Just then Helen interrupted to ask, "Now who are you going to tell me this one is? Both pictures and you look as near alike as three peas in a pod."

Allen scanned the pictures very closely before he replied, "Darned if I know unless it's father in two different pictures." He picked up the picture and turned it over to find the back a blank. "I don't hardly know what to think, there seems to be a different expression emanating from this one. His left eye has a sharp penetrating expression in this one and in the other one the eyes are softer and more appealing."

They playfully removed the pictures one at a time, giving each a name. When no explanation was handy, they filled one out on a separate piece of paper, with a few added special remarks giving each one an important place in the world's history. They soon tired of this pleasing and seemingly effortless kind of play. Helen's face began to appear as if she were in need of sleep as she tried to control the increasing desire to just stretch her arms back in a pleasing and satisfying yawn.

Allen noticed that she was becoming weary, jumped to his feet nearly upsetting the table and reminded, "Come on, wake up, let's finish these pictures. There are only the first three we looked at to finish."

Gouging him one in the ribs to get even, she responded, "Golly, I'm glad you did that, it saved me from showing my weakness, I was surly going to sleep. Alright, this one first, we can call it the professor and give him the credit for knowing what our present system of economy is and the troubles we are having with our political system."

She paused before she continued, "Say Allen, that reminds me. Have you ever wondered why they separate those two functions of government? This spring in school the question came up for debate. Say, did we have a hot time, it lasted about a week."

He had been listening and trying to remember the incident. Having no memory of it he replied, "No, I've never thought much about it, but I do remember the commotion it stirred up for awhile. If you are not too tired, I'd like to hear what you learned about it."

"I couldn't be tired enough to drown my interest in repeating as much as I can of that debate. Come to think of it, even if we have had a long day of it I'm no more tired than you are."

She deliberated a moment then continued, "Let's see, the first question was, 'What does the word politic mean?' Well, we opened the big school dictionary and proceeded to expound its definition pro and con. Finally we accepted the most important. Let's see if I can quote them correctly. 'The art of government or administration of public affairs' was the first one.

The next question on the floor was 'What is government'. This took more dictionary work, we came to the conclusion it must mean 'Party management or control.' Now here is where the fun started. Someone asked the teacher why there were so many parties striving for the management of our government and how were we to know which one could handle the job best?

Now, the teacher could see the whole problem was getting out of her control, so she called in the superintendent to help her. He had been active as a professor for many years and was capable of handling most anything in the form of a debate. He suggested that the most capable pupils be appointed as leaders, one for each political party. Their job was to show why his or her party would be the best able to administer public affairs.

By accident, I suppose, I was chosen to represent the Socialists. This started me to worry for the Socialists Party, although not feared as a party competitor, it wasn't exactly a popular one either.

Well, I had just accepted my task with a heavy heart, when the superintendent pointed toward a small crippled chap by the name of Don, at the time I thought, cruelly unloaded the responsibility and task of representing the very unpopular Communist Party on to him.

My burden now seemed light. I hurried home after school to see if father would help me prepare a short but effective speech for the next day. Now, imagine it if you can. This was the first time I had ever considered a political program from the standpoint of applying it to what I knew of social conditions. Did you ever have anything like that come up in your classes?"

Allen had become deeply absorbed in thinking what he would have done under the same circumstances so it was a moment or two before he could answer, "No, we didn't get into politics very much. On the other hand I had to give a full report on one utopia or another. Some of them are smoothed out nice and pretty, filling a person with hope for a heaven on earth.

I don't know, considering the conditions our political system is in now, I don't believe it is so nice and easy to obtain it the way it is pictured. Especially when you consider the lack of cooperation between one party and the other to bring about such a system of brotherly love and unity."

"That is exactly what I found out, and more too. First let me explain the debate:

First to speak was the Republican. He presented a nice conservative program where if everybody would live within their means and save a little for the future rainy days business would soon come back to normal.

To help balance the budget, we could expand our foreign markets in competition with other countries then use our unemployed at a normal fee to produce more merchandise at a greatly reduced cost. Of course, not in competition to our business in this country but only in the channels of foreign trade.

Most of the blame for the Republican Party's failure to do this satisfactorily he placed on the shoulders of the Democratic Party because they were to liberal in their spending, wrecking the whole financial structure of the country.

The superintendent then called on the Anarchic----Syndicalist. He strode to the front and sharply denounced all politic as useless to the working class common wealth and that the entire production and distribution of the country along with the regulation of justice should be done by the union and it only.

Then came the Democrat. He expounded his belief in a protective tariff with controlled production to meet the back pocket of consumption, conservation camps and back to the land programs for the unemployed. Another fundamental was supplying unlimited amounts of money for borrowing by big controlling companies and substantial banking institutions.

Next came the Fascist.

Say, Allen, are you getting tired of hearing so much political confusion?"

I should say not, I'm still waiting to see what became of the crippled fellow. I wouldn't have blamed him if he hadn't come up with his part."

"Just wait a minute and I will come to him. Oh, yes, next came the Fascist. He claimed all the old parties were doing was maneuvering to lay the blame of failure on someone else.

They did not realize their failure was due to the childish methods by which they promised to accomplish the nations future welfare. What we needed was a leader with enough political foresight and courage to prove to the people that a military dictatorship was for their benefit.

Especially because by force of arms the unemployed could be controlled more easily and the big monopolies could be reduced to government control thereby putting the middle class into power.

Next came my turn, I've told you most of what I had to say. It compared a good deal with the old utopia's of brotherly love, educate the people to vote and finally win the leadership by an overwhelming vote allowing the Socialist Party complete control.

Last but not least came the little crippled fellow named Don:

He limped to the front of the room and stood a moment as though summing up the odds against him then started, 'Comrades and fellow workers there has been much misrepresentation here today, too much to take each separate problem and clear it up for the satisfaction of all of you. So I can only try my best to do it in the short time allotted me.

Under a system supporting profit and private ownership of the means of production, or better known as the Capitalist system, we find an organized system of graft so well developed that by the keen manipulation of it's supporting political parties, it keeps hidden the ugly octopus of exploitation which is pauperizing the entire working class, including the poor farmer.

These parties that have been represented here before you today are all supporters of that cruel monster. They are shorting your life with worry, taking the very food from your tables, planning the cruel enslavement and destruction of your friends and neighbors.

Now, classmates, let's first consider the meaning of government when it's analyzed down to it's true definition;

It means one group governed and another group governing-.

Now, the political party governing represents one group, that group or class that is in power, that plans all it's activity to support its class.

Then the question arises which is the best way to fool the majority and stay in power?

I say it's just like they have done whenever the working class' interest gets traction and builds to the point where it looks dangerous. They just drop the old ways and bring to the front another political party adorned with all the virtues of a heaven sent program full of brand new promises so the working man can hope for the future.

Let's take one party at a time and see what it's objective is:

Starting with the Republican Party: It's program is to save or conserve to the limits of our endurance. Fellow classmates, this cannot be done unless the working class will accept peacefully the dregs of serfdom or the horrors of more capitalist war to exploit the working class of another country.

I believe, you can see that the Republican party is a dead party and it's economy to save the capitalist system is a dead economy.

Next we take the Anarchic----Syndicalist. I don't know why this particular brand is included in our political discussion for it's program is directly opposed to any form of politic. It's theory is based on individual liberty and when judged from our standards of civilization would be chaos. Imagine, if you can, such a condition right here in our classroom.

If each of us demanded our own kind of lessons. Then handled each lesson as we choose.

Could there be order or unity under such a strain?

If not, then how could one gain as an individual or class in such a foolish venture?

We have plenty of such examples here today, just think of our political and benevolent societies of how badly they are divided.

Think of our religious and geographical divisions, it would be impossible to coordinate the entire social problem to a point of perfect harmony unless first, the Communist Party settles the class problem once and for all time.

We will do this by leading to power the working class and establishing the dictatorship of the proletariat.

The Democrat Party in their ventures to reorganize and strengthen the tottering old system have built a crude mythical wall around this country. They are trying to make us, "The People" believe that by hiding ourselves from the rest of the world's commerce, we can live in our own luxurious way. Now, they have forgotten to mention that it is the business interests of our "Capitalist Class", and our exploited colonies which was in the past, and will be again, the excuse to involve the worker's children into another "Capitalist War".

Think of our food supply. How is it that it had been diminished to such a level of scarcity that everyone is becoming concerned?

Of necessity in our struggle to get it, we just naturally enter the market of supply and demand and in so doing force the prices higher. Every time the price goes higher the result is the same as a wage cut, in other words more go hungry. Unless through organized demand, if necessary strikes, the workers need to raise their wages high enough to retrieve their past losses.

The Democrat Party shifts the burden of unemployment another way by placing families on small plots of ground with only partially enough food, tools and seed. Then they tell them, 'Now it is your responsibility to be good citizens and produce enough on this piece of ground to supply your families needs, if you do so in the near future, you may, begin to pay off the price of the land and equipment.'

Fellow class mates, this is serfdom of a worse variety than the ancient land barons could devise. Most of you are aware of men being drafted into the army during the last war. Now, have any of you noticed how, with clock-like precision, in the last three years, the youth of the land have been rounded up in camps and taught military discipline?

Soon to be annexed to the regular army under the subterfuge that we need a larger standing army.

One that the world can look at and fear.

This brings us to the problem of Fascism.

The ambition of the Fascist is to militarize our whole social programs from the very school we are in to the complete determination of all international programs. Everywhere we look we look we see their emblems and preparation coming into view preparing for the real program.

We can plainly see the old parties of capitalism giving way to the vigorous and determined youth of our country, who are, through ignorance of political economy following an aspiring and deceptive leadership in the hope of individual opportunity.

Class-mates, if their program is adopted in this country, we will have one of the worst systems of cast or division of classes in the world's history. Think if you will, of a working class ground down into serfdom or slavery of the worst order, then eking out only a mere existence while under the pugnacious influence of military discipline. Let's not forget while the people suffer the Baron's of industry and finance will be sitting back at ease peacefully enjoying the workers discontent and watching their military puppets protect their country and their molding wealth form being molested.

Then he exposed the Socialist as the super capitalist that uses government to control the people, forcing them to buy from a few companies to enrich the few. Then pacifying them with promises of equality while taking every means of support with numerous rules and regulations that ensure that the few stay in business and power."

Say, Helen, that lad was sure a fiend for politic, that is not the haft of it, how can you remember such a complicated lecture?"

"Well, if your mother and the professor don't come pretty soon I guess I'll have to confess.

Let's see, Don had just explained how the workers would; through militant unions and organized unemployment council support present their demands to gain better working conditions, higher wages and social insurance. With only that degree of improvement in working class improvements they would be able to meet the onslaught of capitalism and expose the political puppets through their protests in militant mass organization.

The superintendent came back from a call, that had taken his attention for quite some time, he noticed the quiet little fellow had won the eager attention of the class, so he paused to listen more intently. Soon a puzzled frown crossed his brow that changed to one of wrath as Don began explaining how some of the conditions imposed upon them in the school could be changed the same way. Angrily the superintendent crossed the room and took hold of Don's arm and bellowed, 'Young man, if your political expression here this afternoon has anything in common with your future purpose and ambition I recommend you be suspended from school. Most certainly, I am going to take your case to the school-board for advisement."

Allen, now intensely interested was about to ask a question when Helen motioned for a moment more time to explain and continued, "Don turned to the class, with determination to see it to the end, appealed to them for a protest against such an outspoken expression of political discrimination.

Well, the class seen in Don's fearlessness an ability to express political ideas that expose the present form of capitalist oppression. The class voted to support him against the superintendents threats.

This support for Don still coming to class lasted about a week. Then one day the superintendent notified him to be at the board meeting that evening. He attended and so did all his class-mates. As the meeting progressed more students from other classes crowded into the small room. This group became a force not to trifle with that caused the school board to back down. So they gave Don a small reprimand and dismissed the matter, so Don could finished the term with high honors."

"I couldn't understand at time how he had overwhelmed them all with his logic. One day I asked him if he would help me to study the lecture from his point of view. We spent many evenings after that in study.

His father would sit in the room reading, if he heard us make a mistake in the lecture meaning, he would jump up and explain certain points then ask us questions. It was not long until in my own way I could give a lecture on the same subject.

Allen now satisfied concerning the young radical, jumped to his feet pulling Helen with him, exclaimed, "Come on, let's go out in the air and stroll awhile."

Chapter XIV

Economic Worries

Slowly, but surely, the time slipped by. The work Allen did with Mr. Harris added to his experience putting him more in contact with the world and life's problems. He now saw a clearer picture of life and the struggles the working man had to go through to take care of the needs of his family.

He found himself in the middle of the building of a monstrous dam that was an effort to fill the valley's need for better methods of allotting and distributing water. He weighed the good this momentous venture would bring over in his mind. He found the return for the average person was so small it only left him in disgust.

At times he wondered why people couldn't see the grafting machine that would be in control of the big dam. The graft going to the politicians would sap the energy out of the people to provide them and their favored few wealth while leaving the working people with only a bare living in return.

He witnessed the example of their exploitation in the driving of the workers during it's construction. Mercilessly they had been driven until in a last final effort to be human they rebelled in a strike, to force higher wages and better conditions. Anxiously he watched their efforts as they shrived to understand each others needs and present their demands in an organized militant manner.

Here he was at last, gazing across miles of murky water that had been checked from it's former freedom. The last several days people had been crowding into the little village camp in preparation for the gala celebration of the completion of the dam. He looked around where he could see most everyone he knew, and many more moving from one place to another enjoying the cool moist air as they chatted or viewed the wonders of the modern construction miracle.

He felt a firm grip on his arm that brought back the memories of a happy comradeship that had steadily matured during the last two years. They had seriously studied the problems of mankind and how the ravages of change had undermined their security of life.

He could see Helen next to him estimating the depth of disappointment or despair this jolly mass of deluded humans would sink when they returned home to meet the problems of increased taxes, confusion of water rights and special assessments. Not to be missed are the new processing taxes, controlled production and the increased need to meet the pressing obligations of the past.

Would these ambitious humans in laziness of mind or ignorance float down the stream of physical pain and mental ease much longer without awakening to the class character of society?

As they leisurely walked along, there would be times when the hand on his arm would tighten, then slowly relax to suggest the passing of some sudden emotion or nerve straining within the vigorous mind and body if Helen. Unwilling to brood longer over his own thoughts yet reluctant to disturb the pleasure of hers, he continued to ponder over the past events of the day.

Having enough of this, he lightly touched her hand to draw attention, then receiving pressure on his arm in return, he glanced into her smiling face and cautiously asked, "Pretty quiet this afternoon are you not? Come, let's rest on these logs while you tell me what you think of all this gaiety."

She gave a slight shrug of her shoulders as if to imply that while summing it up she had became a trifle disheartened, "Sometimes I become a little discouraged, especially when large groups are coaxed together with promises of a good time, plenty of refreshments, and a special treat of public speaking by the states most capable orator.

When these political heroes get through, most everyone will have forgotten their promises of pleasing treats, food, and games to go home with high hopes for the states future. They may never know how easily they were duped, removing any thought of demanding their political leaders do something constructive rather than just talking and acting as if they had the real producing class at heart.

Sometimes I guess I get too sympathetic, I do really feel sorry for some of the folks, don't you?"

"Yes, there's old Pete for instance."

She pointed out a short stooped shouldered fellow wearing a cheap funnel shaped hat, a worn sheepskin lined coat that partially covered a clean patched shirt. The one thing of merit he had on, was a worn pair of blue denim overalls. He purposely folded them a little long, so the cuff would help cover the uppers of the shabby worn out pair of shoes.

"I was over to his place the other day, what I saw nearly upset me. The whole family are all in need of clothes. Their clothes are neatly laundered but almost threadbare, even the patches are getting thin. I found his wife in a friendly mood, crooning one lullaby after another to her young baby while she fixed a belated dinner when a large boy, followed by two robust well developed girls, came in expecting their meal to be served as usual.

That is when the trouble started. The boy claimed he could do more if the girls would stay home and help prepare the meals. The girls expressed a disgust for home drudgery, saying, 'we would rather work out in the field, it is mother's fussing with the baby that delayed our meal.' Well, the quarrel went on until the mother began crying. I felt that it would be best for me to go, when Pete stopped the chiding and asked what I thought about his trouble. He went on to tell me how it never used to be like this, but he couldn't seem to help matters.

There was so much work to be done that it took all five of them to take care of the crops and stock. When fall harvest came, they hardly had enough to pay their expenses.

Helen had been listening and comparing their life with the many homes she had visited lately, "Yes, Allen, that's one good example of the depression, I believe is is affecting fifty percent of the homes in this country in the same way.

I had just such an experience at Jenny's the other day. You know, they used to be pretty well off, I enjoyed the afternoon listening to their dreams of better days as they planned one trip after another for their summer vacations. A stranger, not acquainted with the condition brought on by the depression, would have thought these were just normal times, unless, he had stayed to witness the evenings round of contention.

First, the boys wanted money for the dance, including enough for gas and other minor accessories. Then Jenny, thinking she was being left out, appealed for her share of the months budget, this all being settled, Jenny's mother suggested her father take her to the opera. By this time the flush of embarrassment had left his face to express real anguish. I felt ashamed at having allowed myself to be so easily used to embarrass him. This feeling of pity increased when he gave vent to his feelings and told the family that their financial standing was zero. For all he knew there was not a dollar in the house to live on.

Well, I left, but I could still hear them accusing one another until I reached the street. Next day Jenny came down to see me and apologized.

She said her father had killed himself and was to be buried a day or two latter."

They directed their attention away from these troubles to the milling crowd of people that listened to the expounders of prosperity. Allen noticed some that appeared to be disgusted and moved away from the center of the crowd. Among this discouraged few was Pete, gazing about as though to find something of more interest. He recognized the young pair sitting leisurely enjoying the pleasantry of the landscape and hastened to great them.

Allen cautioned, "Here comes Pete, let's find out how he feels about all that is going on today."

From beneath a slouch hat, his friendly voice called, "Hello, folks, how is it you are not interested in the speech making?"

Allen answered, "I don't believe many of the their promises to be true, as for helping me financially, the big dam is a blank. How do you feel about it?"

Pete shifted from one foot to the other a moment or two before dryly beginning, "Folks, I don't know anything for sure, I used to enjoy listening to speeches. Afterwards I would go home to see if there is anything of importance in their idea of the future. I'd change my tactics of farming hoping their advice would get me enough ahead of the majority to reap a good profit.

In the last two years I have become so darn hard-up, I'll soon lose the old home, that is, if I don't find some way to make a profit. I've listened to several of those speakers today." He pointed toward a sleek, well dressed fellow who carried the air of authority, "They just sound flat, I can't see a darn thing worth while in what they've said. Can you?"

Allen scrutinized his face closely and then replied, "Pete, I believe you're sincere alright, but I don't believe you could stand to hear the truth about your troubles."

Alert now, with a serious expression on his face he responded, "I don't care how it hurts. I'd like to know what's the trouble with the whole darn country, You talk and I will listen."

"Well, sir, it starts away back, in the baby-hood when there is first consciousnesses. You saw it happen I know, the baby learns to cry for things, the mother honors it's cry first this way and that. The baby then discover there are others of whom it can take advantage of. Soon taking advantage becomes a regular occurrence to the point he never expects anyone to appose him. As he grows he leaves the protective reach of mother and home. Where he meets the competitive genius of others, where he gets a taste of that old natural law; "survival of the fittest."

Possibly the fight begins with a quarrel over marbles, tops or any number of excuses. He may be the winner of the fight for supremacy, that gives him the confidence to pursue life in the ancient medieval way of depending on his individual strength and endurance to gain a living. Thus being recognized within the farming community, village or city of his choice. This efforts makes him an easy victim for the parasitic minority who, because of lack of intelligence or morals learn the crafty, scheming way of cheating the unsuspecting public to gain their undeserved living.

These have master-minds that apply the art of industry and culture, through political control, upon the whole of society, sapping it's wealth by controlling the worker's labor power."

Pete waited for a pause in Allen's explanation, "yes, I can see part, at least, of what you have said but how do you account for my troubles? I can't seem to apply my troubles to any of these. I haven't been involved in many fights or recognized with the crafty group. I have just tried to make mine by working with nature to do her best for me."

"Well, Pete, I hate to do it but you insist, so here goes. In the first place I didn't mean to imply there's only crafty or physical marvels, for there are both in life. Many people strive for an advantage over his fellows while assuming the outward appearance of a sympathetic brotherly helper.

Now, take the better-than-average farmer. He accumulated his first property either by inheritance, gift or crafty manipulation in a business way. Now take this once well to do farmer I know, a few years ago this farmer worked alone, building a model ranch. Times were good for there was a growing demand for the things he raised. Eventually he met a good looking young lady whose folks were in a very poor circumstances. Her father wasn't able to make a living even though he kept his nose to the grindstone so he became very cross and discontented.

Well, it wasn't long until this prosperous young farmer and she were married. Years passed, leaving them a reward of two grown girls, one husky man, a thriving farm with a good store of stock and a goodly sum laid away for the future in the form of first mortgages secured by some of the best land in the settlement.

When the crash came it became evident the farm wouldn't pay it's own way or pay for extra help. So the conservative farmer reduced his expenses by letting one of the men go. This resulted in the work piling up so he called the boy home from college to help. His careful planning didn't offset the decline in prices. So two more men were dismissed and the girls were called home from school to help in the fields. Now in order to meet their ever increasing taxes and dropping market prices the whole farm had to be planted to hand worked crops.

The cost of machinery was now so prohibitive he could no longer replace or repair it, forcing the family to serfdom or actual slavery because they all had to work sixteen hours a day to complete the many back-breaking tasks associated with intensified farming. This lowering of their social level and hard work left them little time to study or think of a way out so they just increased their faith in the old traditions.

They only had empty hope that the old traditions would assert themselves to the families economic advantage. Hunger the old driving force of all life was now settling in, for they were selling the food they raised on the farm to meet obligations. This left little to put on the table to eat. The family was now afflicted with internal strife, blaming each other and hate now taking the place of the old traditions of love. This left a young girl disappointed, because she realized it was for the want of food, clothing and shelter she married the prosperous young man in the first place. Her many years of work for her family was now rewarded by the reproof hurled at her with burning hate by the family she served.

This overwhelmed her at first but with grim determination and study she found the workers way out. She could see the price of that over-taught dream of love that tempted her, had hidden the real life that is the common lot of all human existence: food, shelter and desire."

As Helen listened to Allen's explanation of Pete's troubles she envisioned the young Pete of other days. Ambitiously taking over the family homestead, with businesslike skill operated the old farm to his advantage. The rest of the family because of continuous quarrels left him in a position to gain complete control. Day after day, he bartered for the accumulated fertilizer from his neighbors farms to enrich the soil of his own. This increased the productivity of his own farm while at the same time decreased the that of his neighbors.

He never consider why he had to do this.

The angry voice of Pete suddenly drew her attention to the two men's argument, "Yes, I admit all these things are true, but, they are legal and recognized as the business part of our civilization."

"Pete, you believe you own your property don't you?"

"Yes I do."

"It's not clear of debts is it?"

"Yes, I won the deed. The only debt I owe is to the bank on a personal loan."

"Then why do you have to plant the whole farm in crop? Why don't you just raise that which is easiest produced and live on your past savings? Sell the mortgages you have, or in other words let your past profits carry you through the balance of your days."

"I have sold and traded those mortgages, but not to my advantage. I had to discount them nearly fifty percent and turn the balances in to meet the last two years accrued expense. Of course, in moving them I added more stock to the farm and improved the buildings some. The taxes have increased so darn much-- even part of last years payments on the crops are still due me. I just can't keep out of debt. I just don't get the money for my crops, no matter how much I raise. Right now the prices are so low that I am about crazy trying to figure how to save enough food at home to keep us eating."

"Now as far as you owning private property, your ownership is just as mythical as it was with the mortgages. All the big financiers have to do is just cheapen the price of your farm produce and raise the cost of it's transportation a little more.

Your private property will soon dwindle to a small piece of land, and very soon with a small mortgage that will increase until the final collapse of ownership into bankruptcy.

Don't you know? It is odd but true, nearly every farmer and most other workers believe they can remain independent of others and still maintain an existence, but in reality they can't.

Take for example your own case. At one time you tried to accumulate profits by exploiting other workers, now you find that in reality you are simply one of them under a misguided illusion. Your profits, you made in the past, are all gone, now all you can do is bid against every other farmer to sell your labor power to the owner.

Under our present social system there is no market for your labor. The difference in the price of labor and labor power is retained by the exploiter in the form of profits. Thus to be accumulated and once more become capital, to used again to exploit workers. Pete, the old political games of business are played out. The old species of life is dying. Soon both will be dead. Which side are you going to be on? The one that's dying along with the old people that are trying to save the old traditions or with the younger generation that is meeting the changing conditions with a new and far better way of living in a workers civilization?"

"Allen, I can't help but believe part of what you have said, but folks, I'll have to be going for the wife will want to go home by now."

Waving farewell he sauntered on across the dam.

"Helen, don't you know I believe Pete would wake up and see what's the trouble if it wasn't for having so much free help at home, say, do they work."

Chapter XV

A Sudden Fling With Nature

They followed the wandering figure of Pete with their eyes for a moment then leaned over the barrier to peer into the yawning chasm far below that was now partially hidden by the deepening shadows of the mountains. Even in the shadow the changes made to the canyon floor by the jagged waste rock that was pushed away from the dam site was still apparent. The sensation caused by the lifting breeze made one feel a ting of fear that a slip would bring an ugly death below.

Suddenly they were thrown to their knees when violent quivers shook the monstrous dam. Fear gripped them when they witnessed the accumulated miles of restless water starting to break through the concrete and steel of the huge dam. In moments the calm waters changed into a surging rush rending the walls of the once mighty barrier.

Allen's eyes bulged from the strain as he desperately clung to the protecting rail.

Helen's started scream was muted by the deafening roar of water rushing through the widening gap in the huge,weakened wall. Part of it to groan then swung open like a giant gate on rusty hinges, causing her to loose her grip and tumble to the edge to start the long decent to the rocks below, but to her relief she felt strong legs catch her and securely tighten about her.

Sickened by the dizzy speed of events and thundering noise, Allen weakly drew Helen to him while below the mighty wall of rushing water boomed and bellowed while it trimmed away the canyon wall in its rush to be free.

They drew closer together in fear, feeling the halting shutter of the flood gate as it balanced majestically about to fall. Their hearts beat faster as they moved with unnerved muscles that ached at the sudden change.

All hope failed as the surging water again carried the ponderous mass, causing the flood gate to lean more precariously. The thundering and booming increased when the mighty waters carried the weakened wall down the raging stream. With white lips they determinedly clung to the rail on top of the solid concrete gate upon which they were grossly imperiled. Slowly it ceased to tip then settled to a jerky stop as the rushing waters receded.

Allen emitted an exultant cry of joy, then wondered at the muted words, for the tremendous noise of the water had covered all other sounds. He glanced toward Helen with an encouraging smile, thankful for the warning noise that had saved their puny lives.

Allen inspected the scene to see if the danger had really subsided. Their clammy fear of possible disaster was renewed by the sight of a funnel of water towards the center of the ancient gorge that was sucking down loose debris.

He motioned for Helen to come with him as he climbed to the lower end of the giant block of concrete. Below was the twisted mass of construction steel with dashing spray glistening in the sun, wet from small rivers of surging water that would make escape precarious. They swung down the twisted steel to where they could consider the last few feet of the drop. Now the journey was over slippery rocks, between spraying surges of foamy gray.

With a resounding splash the race was on. Hearts pounded while nauseating spray taxed their over-worked lungs, while soggy clothes tugged at their stiffened legs, they laboriously helped each other the rocks in the gully.

The sense of an approaching danger whispered as they peered through the mist at the rolling and bubbling water. With new vigor they hurried as if fate was attempting to seal their doom one more time. But, no, with one great effort they held hands and lunged for a projecting rock. Helen was thrown into the air but Allen grimly held on as water poured over him in torrents smothering and choking him as the water level rose then suddenly it ceased to be. Now, he could only feel the tugging of Helen's body that was swaying and jerking about. He was only half conscious as he spent the the last of his strength to bring her to dry land.

The warm sun played pleasantly on his upturned face, it flamed into his eyes searing the very debts of his brain. He struggled to rise, aggravated by fits of coughing and sharp pains that shot through his head and chest. Gentle sympathetic hands eased him back to rest. Gradually thoughts began to formulate: Where was he? How did he get here? All these seemed vague in comparison to the drumming and booming of the mad free water seeking it's natural level to the sea.

Presently he could feel anxious hands soothing his aching brow. He sat up, now he could see the dizzy confusion of the world come into focus, the view he most appreciated was the anxious happy face of his pal.

He held onto Helen's arm for support as he rose slowly to his feet and surveyed the slippery path of their recent escape with wonder. It dawned on him from their recent adventure the reality of the destructive forces of nature.

Where a short time ago stood the majestic wall of security now stood only short projections, between these out-jutting sentinels flowed the remains of the water that once filled the lake behind the dam.

Suddenly horror gripped him as he thought of the disaster in the village below. He was comforted by the thought that his mother and the and the professor had left for the coast a week ago and Mr. Harris had come with them. But what of Helen's mother?

He tried to talk, but he couldn't get the words to come so he motioned a hurried, "Come on" together the wet bedraggled pair climbed the steep hill. As they climbed they each consoled the other in a heart-felt way. They paused a moment while a thrill of understanding possessed them, they studied each other and pondered the recent events.

Voices now became audible as they approached the sorrowing group of frightened people that were gathered above the level of the recent dam. Allen gave Helen a reassuring pat as he persuaded, "Come on, dear, let's find out what is happening here."

They mixed with the excited crowd and listened to the exiting but gruesome tales of woe. Many were missing, no one seemed to know where or how. A few could be seen huddled together on the opposite side of the once water filled chasm.

Those that were missing friends and loved-ones were hopefully studying the faces of the various groups. Others mourned with bitter disappointment in the destruction of the only road. All were pitiful in their worried plight.

Helen became worried when in answer to her inquiry for her father she learned that he had left on foot to go over the mountain trail. Allen reassured her that he knew the trail and would be alright.

Helen's concern for her father was replaced with a new worry when she heard one of the "speakers of the day," that had huddled together in their sudden fright, remark, "I'm sure it'll be a mess down below, I believe we can make a better impression if we leave the poor fishes here while one of us go down to send a relief party from town, use the common herd."

A burning anger took possession of Allen that he roughly expresses in loud acclaim, "Leaders--- great men-- --heroes--- it's a dirty shame that the first thing you can think of is using the masses for your own aggrandizement. Better you realize your own position and assume it's full responsibility, for today is the test of your ability to serve.

Why don't you be finding ways and means of moving these people?

Nice talk you've made today. Now in time of disaster you console them with prayer and nice promises of relief.

Pray, yes, if you want to, relief, yes, if you can get it. But passively hope, no!

Those folks below are in as bad of position or worst then we are."

He then turned from the belittled politicians, before they could recover from their surprise, he faced the gathering crowd and again accused the scheming men who under protest where slinking into the milling crowd.

The partially revived group of people now turned their questioning gaze to hear, "Let's get organized to get out of here. We can find a place more accessible to relief, it will be darn chilly up here tonight. If we can all reach the valley there will be less suffering from the cold."

He held up his hand to again silence the questioning group and continued, "Most of you know the old Indian trail over the hill."

A nod of acknowledgment met his gaze as he continued, "I believe, if we are careful, that with ropes and chains, combined with everybody's help we can make it to town."

A general commotion started as the new idea took shape in their minds. Soon all the cars were lined-up with their load of people to begin the climb over the long forgotten pass. Two lonely sentinels remained only meagerly prepared to keep a fire going all night, in a last hope, that some of the lost, who may be wondering about, might see the light and survive.

Allen could see that the excitement of the dangerous adventure had united them in working for the safety of all. With much effort the loaded string of hapless cars wound a tedious way toward home.

Once they were past the projection of the mountain to a point where they could see the valley below, the caravan halted to view the glistening miles of destruction. The scene was sickening to view, their shattered hopes were replaced with fear. Slowly they became conscious that their homes were now inundated, stock destroyed and loved ones gone. This realization of their loss brought panic and despair. Helplessly they left their cars and wandered about.

Helen in her sympathetic way consoled a small group of mothers, while Allen studied the sorrowful affair while formulating a plan of action. He systematically sauntered about quieting, as much as possible, the others fear.

Once their utter despair partially quieted, Allen, stepped to the fender of the nearest car and carefully began. "friends, we made a journey over the mountain safely by everyone's hearty cooperation, now we're still in a serious situation. There is no use kidding ourselves, we can't live on hope or plans for the future. It takes substantial good food and shelter to keep us fit to meet these hazardous fits of nature.

Now, folks, there are two ways we can cope with our perilous situation:

One: we as best we can make a camp in our present location and send to the county seat for help.

Two: we can elect a committee and a spokesman, chosen from our midst, to represent us in an appeal for help.

This way we can go the county seat in an organized body. Folks, I advise we think it over for a little while and discuss the subject pro and con. It's bound to be helpful to consider each others views, especially on such a serious question."

At this point in his speech a rather over dressed heavy fellow stepped to the fender of the adjoining car, causing it to sway heavily to one side. With eloquent gestures and bitter retorts, played the young adventurer for his lack of experience and self-contained importance.

He paused to measure the weight of his argument and totally misunderstood the silence of so many people that were intently staring at him. He continued to admonish them, as patriotic citizens with faith in the country's future, to scatter out among the farms and villages to better equalize the burden of relief. Of course, this was only an emergency program until they they could be returned to their homes and farms.

Each worried member of the resting caravan, remembered the passive advice of this same speaker during their earlier plight,responded to his attack with persistent booing.

The speaker dismounted with a sneering smile, he had confused the dejected people in their relief program. He was like all puppets of a wealthy master, he had turned them aside. He gloated as he envisioned the hapless band scattered to the four winds burdening the poor to feed them.

Allen listened with intense interest to the orator's attack on him. He became filled with a desire to apologize for his error.

When the speaker continued Allen envisioned the destitute conditions of the already overburdened farming community being stormed for relief by the refugees of the devastated area. The intentions of the speaker now became clear to him, the group was being deceived in an attempt to disorganize them and throw the responsibility upon the poor disheartened people of the flood missed neighborhoods. A surge of anger overcame his passiveness.

Once the other speaker grudgingly left his position Allen spoke once more, "Folks, I believe we're all able to analyze the position taken by our other speaker. He has very little in common with the rest of us. If I understand his position, he still has a place to return to so he is not depending on any relief program to live.

According to his way of looking at the situation, we will be running around hunting for a place to get food and shelter, while he sits down to a well filled table in his comfortable home, satisfied that his two hundred dollar salary was well earned."

Cheer after cheer clearly defined the feelings of the crowd as he hurriedly stepped to the ground.

His position on the fender was quickly taken by a sad faced individual who sharply reminded, "The sun is getting low and my family is hungry. Let's select the committee and get going."

A cry arose for Allen as spokesman. No opposition was offered, so he and four other volunteers were elected.

Chapter XVI

Struggle For Existence

They came to a stop at the curb of the county building, the unfamiliar sight of so many dusty cars drew the questioning gaze of the loitering crowds. There among them in pairs and apparently without purpose were a dozen officers of the law.

Allen was followed by a timid committee to a building with a large conspicuously placed sign that read SHERIFF. From under the sigh emerged a smiling broad-shouldered figure who advanced toward them.

Allen wondered about the number of deputies about the place as he determinedly stepped forward to meet the sheriff.

With calm steady words, Allen gave a short description of the disaster, then motioning to the parked caravan he continued, "This homeless and destitute group are making an appeal to this county for relief. We are the acting committee and can handle the business accordingly."

The Sheriff smoothed his hands together, the sympathy in his voice was appalling as he sadly expressed, "Now, that's too bad, I'm sure we can fix you folks right up, Now, let's drive right down to the relief station."

He glanced at his watch and continued, "Better we hurry though, it will soon be closed, you folks just follow my car and we will soon be there."

With renewed hope the waiting families received the committee's report. In an unbroken line the fifty cars, like a funeral procession, made their way to the relief station.

People were gathered in a score or more of waiting lines that were swelled by the added numbers of the newcomers slowing the progress because of the added numbers. The small committee followed the sheriff through the spacious building to be intercepted by an aged individual with pencil and tablet in hand.

The sheriff asked the authoritative person a few questions then turned to Allen and instructed, "We will have to wait a little while so you boys just sit down until this gentleman," he pointed to an aged gentleman, "Calls you, then go right into his office and present your case to the county matron."

He glanced several times at his watch as he continued, "I'll have to run along, if I'm needed have them call me on the phone and I'll do everything I can."

He smiled again as he caressed and smoothed his big hands together, bid them adieu and left.

The hour wait ruffled Allen's nerves to the breaking point suddenly he was startled by a gruff voice, "you're next."

He looked around to discover the aged man standing in the doorway impatiently pointing towards him.

Encouraged they stepped though the entrance where they were abruptly halted. "Only one at a time."

"We are a committee representing a stranded group of people."

"I can't break the rules here."

He continued his protest but it became of no avail so the argument closed as the old man closed the door and reminded, "You heard what I said, one at a time or not at all."

They stepped back for a moment in their confusing just as a dark young fellow with cold penetrating eyes walked up to the old man and commanded, "Get out of our way these people are in a tough spot."

The old gentleman was reluctant to move but was soon firmly pushed aside by the young man so they could pass to the matrons desk where Allen once again repeated their plea for relief.

Lines of worry crossed the matrons face, apparently she was mortified at the sorrowful story. The buxom lady rose with an expression of sympathy as she replied, "I'm sorry folks this is entirely out of the question. Our budget will hardly take care of those we already have on the rolls. Haven't you folks some friends or relatives with whom you can stay for awhile?"

Allen's heart began t sink as he became aware of the smooth way the sheriff had passed them along just to be put off until some other time.

The matron glanced at her watch and sharply remarked,"Now, folks, if you will step out side please, I have a good number to see yet this evening."

"Yes, but we have no place to go, we've got to have food and a place to go."

"Now, gentlemen, if you were citizens of this county we would have to make some kind of arrangements. You have to live in the county six months before we can consider your case. Good-day."

Allen was in a daze as he tried to fathom the matrons point of view. He now, could see the bankruptcy of the system, how could a mind be so badly warped. Nearly everyone in the group were citizens of the county. Taxpayers to both the government and the state.

Everyone of them had actually lived all their lives in a neighboring county in the state.

Why were they not citizens?"

Why couldn't they have relief?

Could she consciously be an enemy of the proletariat or just one whose mind is entirely controlled by her meager salary paid by the economic interest of the ruling capital?

The importance of the occasion began to take shape in his mind. He felt this responsibility was more than he could bare. He wondered if his followers were the only ones under this terrible dread, or if this attitude explains the presence of so many other desperate people in the building?

His heart was heavy as they returned to the others to deliver the sad report.

On the way back to the the room where the main body waited he scanned the desperate faces of the members of the committee, there he found no help in solving their immediate needs.

In a last effort he went up a few steps on the stairs and raised his voice so that all could hear. "Folks, it seems as though we are not citizens of this county, for that reason, they tell us we can expect no relief.

I would like to ask a question of those that live here. Is there any other organization we can turn to for aid?"

"Yes," came a clear firm voice from near where he stood, "There is one such organization, of that I am a representative. If you, and those whom you represent, are willing to except our aid we will act."

He recognized the same dark eyed youth who had already shown his willingness to help, "Friend," he explained, "I am sure, if you will, that your actions will be greatly appreciated by all of us."

"Then," began the youth, "I am sure, we can gain our point without leaving this building,"

With this he ascended the stairway, to a point where he could be seen by all and inquired, "How many neighborhood captains are present?"

Immediately half-a-dozen hands were fluttering above the crowd.

"Friends" he spoke seemingly to those who raised their hands, "We are in need of mass support."

His words seemed to have immediate effect. Several men and

women began worming their way toward the door in an effort to leave the building for help.

In a few minutes the door began to swing almost continuously as small groups entered to join those who were already present. Soon the room and sidewalk became jammed as a result of the neighborhood captain's work.

Apparently the organization was being called together swelling the crowd. The youth continued to speak with appreciation for the helpers, "Friends, this building proudly displays the sign: RELIEF TO THE NEEDY, but we have learned by experience that relief must be forced from them by our own organized efforts. There will probably be a little confusion, I may be taken out by the law. But, if so, someone else will take my place. Do not be worried if several of us are arrested, for hundreds more are coming to your support, they can not stop us. This struggle will continue by increasing mass support until we get results."

Gradually the sad faces of Allen's own party began to show signs of interest and determination. When the speaker finished three very official looking men appeared at the top of the stairs.

The faces of the men showed signs of worry as their spokesman asked, "How many of you are there in your destitute group?"

The militant youth glanced a questioning look toward Allen for an answer. "I don't know for sure, there must be near two hundred."

The official spokesman did not change his expression as he continued, "That is too many for us to find houses for right now, but we have located a vacant rooming house that would accommodate you all. If that will do?"

"We might accept that for the present." answered the dark-eyed youth, "What about food relief, these people must eat?"

The official spokesman looked at the dark-eyed youth questioningly as he spoke, "I think that can be arranged. I will call several storehouses and place your orders, but with a certain limit."

With this he handed the youth a sheet of paper upon which was written the address of their new home.

Chapter XVII

Father's Warning

Helen sat gazing from the window of an ancient, yet serviceable rooming house reflecting on recent events. In the park below the restless neighborhood youths walked, played or rested expressing the thrill of being alive. Their experiences both pleasure and disappointment becoming their schoolmaster of life.

In contrast to the flitting life below, her father thoughtfully sat rocking. He was tired and heartsick from the long search for his mate that resulted in only finding her silent form.

The creaking of the worn stairway aroused his attention, "Where is Allen? I haven't seen him about this afternoon."

Helen turned to her father to reply, "He is out with Bert getting acquainted and hunting for new ideas, they'll be here most any minute for supper."

Now with interest he moved his eyes around the poorly furnished but clean room, apparently unsatisfied he continued, "Who is this Bert?"

Then as if it just occurred to him ask, "What about that supper? I haven't seen a home cooked meal since yesterday."

In response to his question a gong's musical note sounded throughout the building.

She arose and encouraged, "We'll have to hurry and wash up, for we eat in fifteen minutes."

They washed up and were about to go down for supper when the young men returned, slightly astonished at their sudden appearance Helen gathered her wits and introduced, "Father this is Bert, he helped us in organizing to get our relief home."

The introductions completed the small group repaired to the dining-room.

With very little confusion the two hundred people took their places at the table. Order was enforced at the tables crowded by children by a few women that reminded them to be quiet. At the end of the room a young man rose to speak, "We will have a few encouraging words from our co-worker Bert."

The Dark young man coolly stepped on top of an empty box and spoke, "I have been asked to explain a little of background on our organization and how we managed to acquire this community home. Party members are always working among the people, organizing and collecting them together to help them understand how a worker's government functions. Once we understanding man's nature we can advance toward the new and higher civilization.

Every branch of the organization has been built upon the basis of necessity, just as this home is a necessity. In the past working people have just existed, now it is time to awaken to our greater responsibility. To-night at eight o'clock there will be a meeting in this room, the purpose of this meeting is to discuss ways to better coordinate our work."

With no other ceremony he quickly joined the others in the evening meal.

Adjusted somewhat to communal life and with a better appreciation of each others efforts they heartily consumed the course but satisfying food.

Later that evening Allen stood in the doorway of the big room, enjoying the sight of his fellow unfortunates taking the responsibility of directing and clearing the aftermath of the meal away in preparation for the expected meeting. He was touched with sincere sympathy when his eyes fell upon Helen who was bravely facing her sorrow, her eyes made bright, by gathering tears that were surfacing. She was striving to "Carry-On" by cheering others who were carrying burdens similar to her own.

"Come," Allen spoke soothingly as he approached, "You are free from duty until early morning. We have an hour before the meeting---- Let's stroll in the evening air, it may make things seem a little brighter as we talk. We have been too busy to even notice each other since---- we came to the city.

Her smile was obviously forced in an effort to restrain her feelings.

"Yes", she agreed, "It might help, sometimes, I feel almost faint. When I think of tomorrow it seems so unreal I can hardly believe ------."

"Come pal", he admonished in an effort to help in her fight for self-control, "We've got work to do and others to think of----let's talk out under the trees."

This had its strengthening effect, her smile came now with more genuine ease as they moved on into the park.

"You're a real pal, Allen, one a person can depend on when they need a friend."

"Don't be to sure," he teased, "I might have ulterior motives, I may be plotting to satisfy my own greed and lust in the future. Who can tell?

Besides, my ability wouldn't have amounted to very much if Bert hadn't come to the rescue."

"Yes, that reminds me," Helen began, "If you're though joking about how barbarous you are, I feel kind of out of place, there's just something about all this." Motioning toward the rooming-house, "I mean this home-and-food. I thought we studied all about the class struggle to exist, but when it actually happens---well, I just don't understand."

"You're not the only one, all of us are mighty appreciative and probably more puzzled about how it is done than you are. In fact, that's why Bert has agreed to explain everything he can to us tonight." Then as if on second thought he went on, "Oh, you know, when Bert and I went uptown this afternoon?" He waited a short interval for her to reply in the affirmative he continued, "We went to City Hall, Bert told the city officials just what he was going to do tonight. That he's going to expose their program of exploitation and hunger, he even invited them to come tonight to defend themselves.

He told me this afternoon that he didn't think they would come because they are so secure in their office they will just laugh it off."

Helen remained very quiet and thoughtful for a moment before she spoke, "Speaking of mysteries, that young man is just as mysterious as his deeds. Imagine--a total stranger coming to our aid, no pay--certainly not an "Ulterior Motive." I've read of such men in books, but you certainly don't expect to meet them in real life, Can you explain why he has done this for us?"

"Say," exclaimed Allen, "You'll be asking if he is married next--no, I can't tell you why he did it, I'm wondering if having a competitor is worth the benefits or not."

With this they enjoyed a hearty laugh and started on their way back to the large room where their questions would soon be answered.

Almost every one from the big home was there. Some seemed nervous, twisting about to notice each new comer as they entered.

Allen looked about then quietly leaned over and whispered softly to Helen, "He's here," then settled back to wait for the meeting to begin.

Bert briskly stepped to the front and began, "First we will have to appoint a secretary and chairman."

Once a chairman and secretary were appointed, the newly elected young chairman rose and remarked, "Co-worker Bert is here tonight to challenge the integrity of the city officials. They were to come here to defend their meager distribution of relief. If they are here to defend themselves, we would like them to come forward." He hesitated for a moment, no one responded so he continued. "There is no response. So, I will turn the time over to Bert to explain our position in this struggle for an existence.

Bert stood up and seriously studied the door for a moment before he spoke, "I asked them to be here. I am sure their expressed intentions to help us are not sincere or they would have come. So, we just as well begin. Getting a living is the most serious task of the employed and unemployed. Each idol person has a question of how to obtain that living. Each family has the same problem: Hungry children crying for bread and landlords pounding on the door for money. When neither is available, how then, do you think is the best way to obtain both?"

The expressions in the serious group could not be taken lightly for they ranged from passive or submissive due to their faith to destructive through terror.

Each member of the crowd was allowed to express his ideas, when those that stepped forward were done, Bert still studying a list in his hand rose, "Now, I have here about twenty different ways this group has expressed it can be done. That means we should divide into twenty different gangs, then have each gang do their determined best to win over the others to their point of view."

While Bert paused to weigh his next remark, Allen envisioned the gangsters of the day fighting among themselves for special privileges to prey on society, each smaller gang "rubbed out" because of the ambition of the larger to impose their power over the rest.

Once Bert was satisfied with the effect his last remarks had on the audience he continued, "Now it is plain to see we can't achieve our purpose this way. This is how the owner's of this country have enslaved the working class. Using monetary control of our property, deeds, mortgages, bonds etc. they have spit us into opposing groups. Figuring while one is worried about payment of a deed, another concern will be the foreclosure of a mortgage, while another the shrinkage of his few dollars worth of bonds, others the delusion that they can one day buy a house or become president. This whole while the wealthy class go to warm resorts in the winter and cool mountains in the summer leaving we the workers, the real producers of wealth to toil.

Each of you have slaved for a living ever since you were old enough, turning over the soil, planting and harvesting just the same as any other worker in a factory or mine.

Bert paused and queried," If there is anyone who wants to to ask a question don't let me talk you down, just stand up or raise your hand. I'd like to hear some questions."

As if needing only this little encouragement an interested farmer shouted out, "I'm sure most all of us realize how busy we've been worrying about our own financial problems, instead of questioning the reason why all of us are doing the same thing, now what I want to ask is, how do you explain the farmer being just the same kind of worker as the fellow who works in the factory or mine?

The farmer raises food, while the factory worker or miner toils for wages."

Allen only had a vague understanding of the subject so he listened intently to absorb every point as Bert explained.

"Plainly it would be impossible for any one man to even build a house and furnish it in a lifetime by himself. He would first have to prospect for the ore then refine it to make iron implements. Then go out to cut the timber to make the lumber, then get it home if he could to start on the house while at the same time making a living.

It plainly could only be done by many workers each doing his own task. Some mining the metals and other minerals, to supply the factories that build and shape the tools, implements and other things needed to build the house.

All the while the farmer is raising animals and produce to supply other factories where they are processed to feed more workers.

His thoughts were interrupted by a nudge from Helen who thought he was loosing interest. He started to speak but she put her finger to her lips as she glanced toward the speaker. Now disturbed it was a moment before Allen settled down again to listen.

Bert paused a moment to sip some water then continued," On the farms in most every country of the word are men and women of all colors with their families working and sweating to provide food and a place to live. In most very mine or factory we find the same mixture of people toiling together hoping to earn enough to buy food and shelter, It is this kind of exploited worker that produce the necessities of life and are the fundamental part of the working class.

Now, rather a person is black, white, yellow or red it makes no difference they have to live. Now only when he is disgusted with the present system of exploitation and diligently compares it to the new organizational working class way out can he, through struggle, become able to appreciate and later enjoy the new civilization and only then can he actually be called human. The increasing hazards of nature make it necessary for we humans to better understand the world and organize together to live."

A hand shot up and was aggressively shook about, Bert stopped and nodded for a question. A rather tall middle aged man rose and in a slow drawl spoke, "I can see how we farmers have done a lot of hard work for mighty small wages, but there's one important question to settle, how do you bring the white and black man into the same class. I'd like to have this better explained."

Allen enjoyed watching the surprised faces at the ease that Bert had handled each new subject. His mind seemed crammed with answers and a new understanding of the masses in their struggle to survive. In Allen's mind was a continuing broadening picture of people from every part of the earth forced to mix together, carrying on with hope, in a new land, striving for nature's resources. To become a changed people not divided against each other in purpose or fact but united. Instead the ruling class the wealthy exploiters of the masses, becoming worried victims of their own devices, driven on to desperate ends by their fear of their upcoming crash.

It was coming to Allen that understanding alone could not suffice, it would take a struggle led by only working class leaders who opposed the exploiting class to unite the toilers in appreciation of the value of each other.

Allen's thoughts were again interrupted by Bert's voice as he answered another Question, "The human has five senses namely, feeling, taste, smell, hearing and sight. It doesn't matter what color he is, the pleasure or pain he registers from these drives him in his desire to live.

Under the profit system each individual is lead on by his passions----with mental torment his affections lead him on----with endless hope. With the collective thought of organization that has so effectively brought forth results here, can be more indeterminably expressed as it comes into the fighting consciousness of us, the working class as a whole. Then the victory for labor will soon be ours."

Allen pondered the serious events of the day, he was seriously considering a serious change in his economic life and its relationship to his fellow man.

He thought of the one pleasant part of his past that he would keep in his present struggle that was the interested companion at his side, she gave him confidence and a reason for a better life.

Now that his own inner struggle was about settled he listened with intense interest in an effort to learn how this new order worked. There were many questions about the new thought process that would guide this new mode of life. This was also reflected by the crowd, many wouldn't let the meeting end until Bert promised to stay with them to compare ideas. Many indicated they wanted to leave their current imperfect lives in the past and made the new mode of living their future.

Allen motioned to Helen they should leave, the crowd was packed in so tight it was a struggle with both words of apology and physical effort to worm their way out of the building. They avoided much of the crowd by slipping through the kitchen toward the back door on the way Allen commented, "That sure was a good example of working class enthusiasm. It was a lucky break we had, being able to work as an organization to procure food and a place to live."

He stopped speaking when he noticed some men unloading boxes and bags from a truck and putting them in the supply room off the kitchen. He noticed that many of the caned goods were labeled "Deseret" and the bags were printed with "Bishop's Storehouse."

These labels seemed out-of-place in a world where Bert spoke of organizing and demanding that the people in power provide the unfortunates food and shelter. He wondered if everything about their rescue was really the way it was made to look.

They watched the truck disappeared down the back alley before they walked toward the street. Allen asked before he continued, "That's odd, Bert told us his organization forced the county officials to give us food and shelter to my understanding Bishop's provide for the needy, we need to look into this further. Anyway Bert and I were down to the relief station today talking to some of the people down there. One of them said a group of men were coming down to chase us out of town tonight. What do think about it?"

Showing her confidence that they could do no such thing, she replied. "I don't believe they'll have an easy time getting rid of us. We must of hurt the feelings of the town masters when we didn't submit to their abuse----since Bert has taken an active part in helping us to understand our problems. I'll bet, the relief masters are sure fuming because if there is anything they hate to do----it's giving in to the workers with adequate relief. It's a good thing we the workers had a growing organization before we came or I'm afraid we would have gone hungry. Now with our added strength I believe, Bert will have them guessing."

While they peacefully sauntered along their eyes were assailed by an outburst of rude and threatening language. A large sedan pulled up to the curb beside them. Leering half drunk faces were visible through the open window from among them came the familiar voice of Royal.

"Ya cheep cut-in, think you're smart mixing with the reds, don't ya? Well, we had a little bad luck getting' the boys together, or we would have made sausage of the whole----mess of ya tonight."

So sudden had been the verbal attack that Allen's hadn't overcome his surprise when Royal groggily continued, "Do ya know your old man? Well, you thought you didn't have one living did ya? Well, I know the old boy, he changed his name so's ya wouldn't catch on. His name is B. A. Craige, he's been a partner with my dad for years, got another kid too. Say a pretty----you turned out to be."

Allen could control his temple no longer. He flung caution to the wind as he sprang to the car window and in his rage jerked Royal's drunken body half through it.

A cry of pain and fear checked this attack as Royal begged, "Its the truth, I tell ya, let me loose and I'll prove it."

Royal pulled a picture out of his wallet that showed Royal, his father and a man that looked like Allen sitting behind a desk with a name plate that said B.A. Craige.

Allen stared after The Sedan as it pulled away from the curb. He then got another surprise when the car again stopped and a familiar figure piled into the back seat.

What was Bert doing with Royal and his hoodlums? Allen asked himself.

Chapter XVIII

The Family Ghost Returns

Allen was now awkwardly weaving in and out of people along the busy thoroughfare. His mind frenzied by all the recent events, he saw each hurrying person as only a shadow. His mind was in an uproar, as he reviewed the story of his hidden past. He become a slave to his passion as he dwelt on his imaginary loss and grimly clung to his one ray of hope. Every step brought him nearer to the answer.

He didn't remember reaching the dull gray building because his only thought was the hated door. Now out-of-patience with himself for the past delay he quickly turned the knob and strode in.

There at a the desk with several documents in his hand sat the startled object of his search. He scrutinized carefully the once jolly face hoping to discover the cold expression he remembered from his uncle's picture. No, the once lively expression of the eyes were there with only a little sign of inner deception.

He quickly crossed the room to face the silent standing form.

"John Rodak"

The silent man replied showing only a hint of feeling, "Yes, Allen."

Thoroughly confused by his response the youth queried, "You mean you knew I was coming?".

"Yes, Royal threatened to expose me yesterday and I believe I understand a born rat when I see one."

Allen wondered at the artless way, this ordinarily cold businessman had spoken.

Could it be the trick of a scheming mind? But why?

Determined to find out he asked, "Why do you, a businessman, with no scruples in a deal, try to be so frank with me?"

A little taken back by the direct question he answered, "Allen, I have a few things to say to you about that, which I hope you are able to understand.

First, I want you to know, I am not asking for pity or sympathy for I have played the business game and lost. Why should I, a man who has measured the value of life by my income, expect quarter in my last wavering hour."

Allen was in a quandary he tried to shake off the mental fog, by blurting out, "What excuse has Royal to meddle with your family secrets?"

Without a quiver of an eyelash the answer came, "That is part of what I have to tell you, I had better start at the first before you were born, we had better sit down."

He dropped in a chair and motioned for Allen to sit in the other,

Allen was reluctant to further concede his weakness so he retorted, "No, I'll stand here for the present, your expression of how little you value the worker's life prohibits a common understanding between us."

The businessman thoughtfully studied the boy's face as he carefully replied, "I told you how I feel in regard to sympathy and the worker's life, sit down and listen a minute and I'll tell you how cheaply I value human life. First, the worker to me are like worms at a carcass crowding and squirming to devour the most food. However, useful, yes, by selecting the younger and stronger ones they can provide the most labor."

Allen felt that he was no longer subject to compromise so he lowered himself in the big chair to listen.

"Your mother was an innocent small town girl, in love with a fellow named Tom L. Hopkins. He decided to go away so they quarreled. Well, he went away and I courted his girl and we were finally married.

My father always picked at me and gave me the worst of the deal whenever my brother and I were concerned. He gave me a farm, well, it was made up of three farms he had foreclosed on because the previous owners couldn't pay the mortgages. All three were badly run down. Now my brother he gave him a flourishing business here in the city worth ten times as much as the farm.

I hated him for it but there was nothing I could do about it but wait for an opportunity to get even. The more I thought about it the more discontented I became. Secretly I blamed your mother for being an extra burden that kept me down."

Allen was listening for some expression to help him understand his lack of affection or as expressed among the more poorly educated, "Love" in this cold man of desire.

He inquired, "Did you and mother believe you really loved one another at one time?"

Yes, we did, but my passion to be relieved of the irksome labor of the farm soon overruled any such thought. You have such a habit of wanting to know my present thoughts, so I will tell you now to save another interruption. Women from a business standpoint, are a flop. In love they are only a pawn to be used in case of desire. The same as all other life, if they are profitable, now back to where we left off, as if to muddle things up worse, along came the big war and my call to camp. When I went around to see my folks before I left, my twin brother Bill, made me a proposition. He would take my place in the army and I would take his assumed name. Your mother didn't know this.

For a long time things went well. I pulled the business out of the hole and came out well on top. Then came the crash, I had to maneuver my affairs to keep from being ruined. During this time of crisis Royal's father and I met, he and I were in the same strait, so we joined companies.

This relieved the financial tension for a time and brought a fair outlook for the future. Our chance for recovery came when the contract for the dam was announced as ours. Soon afterwards we discovered our mistake, we had underestimated the depth to a solid footing for the dam. We tried to hire your friend Mr. Harris but was already committed. Royal played a certain part but he balled it up.

Yes, I enjoyed his story of defeat. He was a sorry site after you were through with him.

After that I made a deal with Harris for his oil well, it returned a little money but while I was involved in making the oil well produce, Royal and his father took short-cuts on the dam that led to the dam's collapse and the ruin for all of us.

Once it collapsed Royal worked out a new scheme with one of his boys, I think his name was Bert, to use the victims of the dam failure to get money from the government or the victims for him and his father to start over. It all fell apart when the government refused to help and it was left to the churches to provide relief for your friends and neighbors. You may go see that Mormon stake president if you want to know more about that.

Young man, you know the story and it's up to you what you do with it. Royal knew little about my family affairs, but what he does know he won't tell."

Allen shivered at the matter of fact way the story was told, he remembered the slurs of yesterday and inquired, "Royal said I had an illegal half brother, is that a fact?"

"No, The women I lived with had a son before I ever knew her. He was killed in a street riot shortly after their marriage. His wife was killed in a train wreck shortly after the birth of her son. The baby now lives with its grandmother."

The door of the office was flung open with a resounding bang and a ponderous man of forty waddled up to the desk. "Sorry to interrupt you, Craige, I want some advice and I got to have it now."

Allen rose and proceeded to leave, when his admitted father stepped to his side and warned, "Think over what you've been told, make your decision as to how much of this history you want the world to know. I want you to see me tomorrow. Good bye young man."

There was something in the man's farewell that really appealed for an answer but the very difference of principle made him hold his tongue, as he thoughtfully strode from the room to the street below. There was still a tinge of freshness in the morning air that added vigor to his mind and cleared his understanding of the short visit.

This cold heartless man must have been his father, according to the pictures Allen had seen. How could he become so cankered and disgusted with humanity without a reason?

Then flashed into Allen's mind the expression he used concerning Royal "Born Rats" could it be that his contact with this kind of people in business had eventually hardened him?

Could he believe that practically all human beings would sell out life and principle for a few pennies?

Could he not see that the struggle was a clash of classes?

His class the dying one calling for help, doctors for this and doctors for that, to patch it up and cure its aches and pains. While the victims of its death struggle, with determined purpose and fore-warned leadership will built the new civilization to replace the old.

Disgusted with a human who could become such a miserable piece of business machinery and not aware of his plight, Allen hurried on as he meditated, a father, he may have been to some, but only to cover up the slow deceiving process of his business while it ground out the lives of the toiling mass.

Wait a minute what did he say about Bert---- a scheme---- to get money from the government and the victims? How?

Who helped us?

What did he say about the Mormon Stake President?

If in fact the churches helped us, then what about the workers Civilization?

Chapter XIX

Death's Helping Hand

The morning had been one continuous event to Allen, climaxed in the final preparation for the funeral planed for the many victims of the breaking of the dam. Stubbornly he kept a smile on his face with a cheery word for the members of the bereaved families.

The excitement now over he wandered to the small park to rest and think. Life's whirl was crowding in on him too fast. The many questions rolling around in his mind at times overlapped to become only a jumble of confusion. Infinitesimal man, wandering about in this changing orbit, following the old and new traditions in his struggle to survive. Born in agony---creating thought and desire---could it be the birth pangs of the synthetic man in his struggle for existence in an artificial world?

Could it be that in the natural state man was unconscious of kin and only appreciative of only kind?

Was this any reason for lack of affection while in his father's company?

Would the traditions of each epoch change the emotional man to a scientific thinking being?

Life was beginning to be more valuable to Allen than only the appreciating of the binding traditions of a superstitious environment which would drive him deeper into the slavery of one of the serving class.

Or was freedom supporting freely those in need and giving of oneself for the benefit of others?

He was too deeply absorbed in his own thoughts to hear the approaching steps of Helen. He only realized that there were others about when the soft touch of Helen's fingers gently closed about his eyes.

He reached up and clasped one of her hands and coaxed, "Come, dear, I want to talk with you for awhile."

Her hands released from his eyes as he drew her down beside him so he could witness the tear stained eyes of a plucky lass that tried to cheer him up by chiding,

"Trying to hide away with your troubles? You wouldn't give a chance all this morning to talk to you and now that's the very thing you want to do, Come now, speak out. I'm listening." He understood these words were only to cover up her recent emotional outburst of emotion for the loss of her mother. He felt sure, she would not be satisfied until he had explained the outcome of his early morning trip. So with as little emotion as possible he described his father to her.

She became so interested in envisioning this soured, cruel being, for a time an ever changing picture played within her mind. She envisioned him desperately clinging to his hopes of success as each try for wealth lowered his values and sucked him deeper into the sea of debt.

He was determined to struggle on in his deals that ruthlessly destroyed and wasted the human prize, his life. Then, when he felt he was again on his way to the top, he breathed easier, then gradually expanded his passions or desires for pleasure in his own daring and selfish way. She then turned her attention more to Allen's telling of his morning visit, feelings of sympathy drowned all memories of the funeral and those sad preparations from her mind. She could only see the resolute face of Allen as he described his hated experience with his father.

Once finished with this short history he glanced at the sun to see the time of day and warned, "We had better be going, the funeral is to take place in less than an hour."

This returned Helen's thoughts to the memory of her mother that again dampened her partially returned cheerfulness so they appeared a downhearted pair at the end of the short walk to the big building to make the final preparations for the sad event.

The order of the day was confusion as the various family members viewed the many dead lying in their inexpensive, poorly furnished caskets. Several undertakers pressed in the crowd, giving orders in an attempt to keep some sense of order. Policemen whistled to turn the traffic away from the crowed street.

This jumble of emotion and activity finally settled back to peace and quiet as the long string of cars pulled to the curb of the spacious church.

The gathered throng patiently sat with awe and reverence as they listened to the frail attempt of the worldly speakers to console and deride.

In this tight group Allen was able to study many faces as the speakers presented the glory of the peace of death to ease their fears. Perhaps, they would long for such a home of quiet and rest. In their enthusiasm the speakers caused many to compare their meager lives with that hopeful future that sounded so sublime that they partially forgot their traditional lot of pain and woe. As he glanced from face to face he noticed many that had been his fiends since childhood. To his surprise and winning all of his attention was the sight of his mother and the professor thoughtfully watching the proceedings. His thoughts drifted back to the past when he anticipated their timely meeting.

When the services ended he tried to move over by his mother and the professor but they were lost to view in the moving throng. He then returned his thoughts to Helen with her pale face and sobbing eyes that brought a catch in his throat as he mentioned, "I saw mother and the professor a moment ago. We need to find them after we go to the cemetery."

The appeal in her eyes told more than words as she said, "I don't care to go out there. Let's walk instead."

They wandered several blocks with thoughts of current events and the future, when they were startled by a shrill voice at their side, "paper mister. Read about the Craige murder and suicide." He continued to sell the story as Allen unconsciously reached with excitement for a paper. Then it struck him as he drew back with embarrassment and exclaimed, "Sorry, buddy, I'm flat." Then he reached into his shirt pocket and showed him an inexpensive pen as he continued. "Here if you can use it."

The lad knew it was a bargain, quickly took the pen and handed Allen the paper before he strolled on down the street to call his wares. Helen pushed aside her grief to listen carefully to Allen read the gruesome account of his father's revenge. It stated with a few minor details concerning his business and finally climaxed with his own self destruction.

He finished reading then silently studied the blaring headlines. He seemed satisfied as he looked over the paper at Helen and spoke, "I didn't understand him this morning when he told me Royal wouldn't talk, but here is the proof of his statement 'Royal and his three friends were found dead in the car probably killed early last night. Mr. Brinkly was found dead in B.A. Craige's office along-side his dying business partner. All of the deaths were probably due to business failure and revenge.' A nice mess I nearly got into."

Helen placed her hand on his shoulder and warned, "Yes, it's good thing for you it happened just before noon instead of first thing this morning. Remember he warned you of how much of your family history you wanted the world to know. I didn't hear a word of your family or your visit this morning. I believe his past died with him. Don't you?"

Allen studied this problem from every viewpoint. He had been grasping for a way to avoid exposure of their recently learned history for his mother's sake. Then he compared what he just learned about his father with Helen's situation whose mind was still in a whirl of confusion triggered by her mother's passing.

He had prided himself in not allowing sentiment to interfere with the cold facts of man's existence and development. He felt he would be satisfied if he put aside the traditional ties of relationship and consider only that the consciousness of the human is evolution's supreme achievement.

With this settled he could sit back and enjoy the process of the man-made world separating the wheat from the chaff.

He finished his self consultation before he asked, "Helen, what do you think of all this worry and fuss we make of our relatives?

We seem to just do it with no real benefit for ourselves."

"Allen, I appreciate this reminder. I should know better than to give into the passions and affections that are our traditional heritage. In spite of myself this age-old influence exerts itself in my outward expressions."

A humorous wink blossomed through the tears to a new appeal, "Even now, for that timely reminder, I long to kiss you."

Her new expression of frankness took him by surprise. It was only his knowledge that she was nervous of outward showing of affection that made it so he could resisted his own impulse to kiss her right there in the open street.

Instead he made and observation, "You're so changeable today, I think something should be done about it. I remember reading that the new museum would be opening today. I think we should go over there for an hour or two. Don't you?"

Chapter XX

Lineage

As they walked to the old-fashioned building they speculated on the museum's relationship to the development of a new and understanding leadership. When they entered the doorway of the cozy building a greeting was called to them from within, "Come right in, don't bother with formality. We haven't put the sign of welcome up yet, just haven't got around to it."

They accepted the greeting as heartily as it was given, they strode right into a big room to receive a breath-taking surprise. Momentary they stood overcome by the exquisite paintings.

The young fellow that greeted them continued, "We're hardly through with this last part, but it gives a pretty good idea of how it will look."

"This" he said pointing to the incomplete part of the room, "Is the last leaf of the giant book to be opened in this epoch history. It contains the final desperate assault of the toilers as they moved to ward victory in overwhelming all the opposing forces of civilization. Those who resist the change are laid aside like chaff before the wind while the workers collectively build their class civilization for the present and future man."

He paused for a moment as Allen questioned, "Don't you think it would be best to view this from the beginning, instead of looking too far ahead without the proper foundation for our understanding?"

Now acting like he made a mistake in his enthusiasm, the painter replied, "Excuse me for being too hasty with this last painting because it really comes first in my mind. Come, let's begin with the first page in the big book of man's history."

He crossed to a part of the room that had been arranged for classes or meetings, then went on, "The earth's crust is a giant book with many pages, each page contains a layer of sediment containing the remains of life that lived in that period of time with some indication of the conditions under which they had to exist. We will skip all of the earlier layers and skip to where man is first found. This side, "He gave a long sweep of his arm to emphasize that he meant the whole side of the room, "Contains the history of man from his earliest stage of history to his enslavement in the toils of serfdom."

He then stepped to the wall and gave them another surprise by pulling on one of the many ropes that hung there.

Slowly a thin layer from the lower half of the wall tilted out toward them. It lifted up and fit snugly into the upper half of the wall. What a wonderful exhibit it presented. Each giant page that came up revealed a new world. The third page illustrated the dawn of man's existence, or was it man?

In this part of the room, where they began their tour, the creatures that were most abundant either lived in the trees or lumbered about in a stooped position.

More careful scrutiny revealed a huge well-formed male that appeared as a huge protector. To some he came across as a protector but to others he was a source of fear only to be faced in preference to the horrors outside his protective influence.

Helen edged a little closer to Allen as she viewed the specimen of physical strength and prowess that was set up to contrast with the tribes many females. Helen watched this king of his kind imagining him in the jungle roaring with rage, knowing that others feared him by instinct or past encounters.

Careful study of the long painting revealed the transition of many generations, older ones dying off along with their old habits. The young were multiplying to greater numbers and developing more physical strength than the old masters.

Farther along, they stopped in amazement as Allen Exclaimed, "Here is a change of events, the people seem to be in confusion. They are running, howling in fright and huddling in caves. Panic seems to be the order of the day."

Allen walked a little farther on then recognized what was happening, "Now I see what it is, the snow and ice is continuously moving down to the lowlands. Those that don't understand what is happening are perishing while others are moving farther south to avoid the cold. They are led now by a new kind of leader, one whose eyes have a good light in them. One that cares for his fellows and seems to watch for danger around them."

As they traveled they met other tribes that were also struggling in a desperate attempt to survive the biting cold. The leaders diligently watched for danger from the elements and also from other tribes. Sometimes the leaders agreed and united the tribes into a more powerful group, other times they disagreed resulting in battles to the end that left the leadership of the tribe to the surviving younger males.

Allen stepped back to view the whole picture. He could plainly see the long journey south that made it necessary to maintain a more upright posture so they could better see their surroundings and make communication easier.

Thousands of tribes must have moved south as the creeping glaciers pushed them closer together. As they were crowded together their lives changed. They now had free time resulting in idleness and mischief.

Generations passed increasing the population causing them to be crowded together in the millions, desperately striving with one another to live. Often chilling breezes from the north destroyed their food causing scarcity and changing the way they lived.

He was aroused from his thought by Helen's voice, "Here, Allen, if you're through looking at this page, we would like to turn to the next one."

He stammered a willing reply as the painter lowered another giant page of history, "Here we have the tribes collected in what appeared as their last stand during the ice age. Much of the land in the warmer areas of the land became densely populated. No doubt they crowded together on the southern coast making life unbearable for each other."

Allen was sure Helen would keep the painter busy for awhile so he stepped back to get a better view of the second page of the paintings.

He viewed the panorama of confusion before him, he could see the effort that was applied by the group to save this traveling horde. The chilly winds from the north made the warmer lands to the south more inviting. So they filled the land between the oceans and the cold.

As generations passed, a new people developed with new leaders that had different ideas of how to live and a different curiosity of the world. He could see that new leaders must have been born that understood how to build a civilization that would build a defense against the cold and hunger of the old way of living.

His thoughts were again interrupted when the painter lowered the next to last painting. Now he could see the result of these new thinking leaders. They outlined a plan to save a number of the trapped multitude until the ice age passed.

Once the ice began to recede those that took leadership urged the people back on the trail of migration to follow the ice and build anew. In this movement they discovered new ways to build and plan.

These rising leaders, or kings, of men would plot to gain for themselves the pleasantries of life on the backs of the toilers.

His thoughts continued as he envisioned the many traditions that were craftily applied to heckle man and leave him with life and hope of a kind but leaving him toiling in one of the weirdest epochs of history.

He could not help but think of man's present struggle to exist. His mental development forever changed his routine of life and forced him to think and live in an unnatural world of his own making.

He looked at Helen and felt a thrill of his own egotism as he thought of man taking control over all other life on earth. Developing a pride that urged the human being to a better sense of beauty and desire for things that he hope for.

The painter went back to his work leaving Allen and Helen to finish the tour on their own.

Helen noticed in an adjoining room the man that had given the address of the rooming-house to Bert. She urged Allen to follow her to meet him. Allen followed her to the next room where they began a conversation with the stranger. "Hello, I am Allen and this is Helen we met you once before, we were with the victims of the dam disaster that you helped with."

The man stood up and greeted them warmly, "Good to meet you both, yes I remember you were one of the committee that was looking for aid. I apologize that the best we could do was that old rooming-house."

Allen let him know that he was thankful for the help he gave then then asked, "How did you manage to get the food and shelter all together? How long has your workers civilization been operating in this area?"

The man looked a little confused then responded, "Allen, I am President Mill, I preside over the local stake of the LDS Church, the block captains and home teachers reported to their bishop that there had been a disaster, because of the number of people effected the local bishops worked with representatives of the other local churches and the stake leaders to gather enough food and supplies to rescue your group. The rooming-house was vacant and happened to be owned by one of the church members who was willing to offer it for your support."

Now Allen and Helen looked confused as Helen asked, "So was Bert one of your 'block captains'?"

President Mills questioned, "Bert"

"The young man you gave the keys of the rooming-house to"

"I thought he was the leader of your committee"

Both Allen and Helen were surprised at how easily they were taken in by Bert. This last statement confirmed what Allen's father had told him. Now they could both see from a different point of view the workers civilization.

Instead of organizing to take from those in power, these workers organized to provide for the needy from their own stores and hard work to take care of the less fortunate. Filling the dream that both Allen and Helen were looking for but not from a political organization but one of religion and love. One that must have been inspired by God himself. President Mill went on to explain that now the funerals were complete there was a plan to help them rebuild their farms and homes and figure out a way for all of the unfortunate survivors to make a living.

Allen and Helen were taken aback by the outpouring of support from a welcomed and unexpected source of hope for their friends and neighbors.

When he was done with his explanations to the now enthused couple President Mill inquired, "Did you enjoy your visit to this museum."

Allen assured him they did.

He then asked, "What did you like most."

Allen said, "The display of the evolution of man from the trees to modern man."

President Mill then motioned to a photograph on the wall that Allen hadn't noticed earlier, "Look at this. How does it change your thoughts on the evolution of man?"

They looked in wonder at a photograph of several men's foot prints fossilized in the coal that lined a cave. The prints were crossed by the prints of dinosaurs.

Helen and Allen looked at each other. Both pondered in silence all they have been through and learned this last while. That all political organizations seem to be more concerned for their own power rather than the betterment of human kind, men help one another not because they are forced but because of the love of God that they posses and now this one fossil cast a doubt on the very theory of evolution that both of them had studied and accepted as fact. Now they both exclaimed at ounce, "This changes everything."

Allen looked at Helen with wonder as he added the explanation, "Your mother was right after all. Don't that beat all?"

Helen's eyes sparkled as she looked into President Mill's eyes and with gratitude said, "Thank you for all you've done for us and for what you have shown us today."

Then she turned to Allen and added, "It looks like we still have a lot to learn and experience in this, 'Life's Tangled Trail'."

About the Author

Nathan John Bullock was born in December of 1895 in Cache County Utah. He Married Emma S Ellis in 1915. That same year he and his father moved their families to homestead adjacent farms near Pauline Idaho.

When the Great Depression set in the country in 1929 it affected Nathan like many others, he gave his crop and farm to his father and moved to Ogden where he wrote this book and finished raising 9 daughters.

Some in county government considered him a radical because he advocated making the farms that were taken over by the county be made available to farmers that had lost their land and other unemployed to help them make a living in those depressed times.

The story I was told by my aunt is: He and his brother Willis went into the county courthouse to discuss the lands that had been taken over by the county from tax sales. They asked that the lands be leased or otherwise make available to the people in the county that were in need.

The attitude of the county officials upset the two of them so much they both jumped over the counter and confronted the officials noise to noise.

They didn't get anywhere with the county officials but they did make a name for themselves as activists for the downtrodden.

He is know as a rock hound and discoverer of dinosaur bones and other fossils. One of those discoveries was two large Petrified dinosaur eggs that must have weighted 50 pounds each. The professors of geology of his day laughed at him and told him they were just rocks that by chance were kind of shaped like eggs.

To prove he was correct in his assessment of what they were he took on of the eggs, set it up on his rock saw and cut it in half. Sure enough it was apparent from the cross section that it was an egg. The shell with the membranes were very clear with the yoke in the place anyone would expect it should be.

The professors grudgingly agreed that they were eggs but still had a hard time accepting that someone without their credentials could know more about paleontology than they.

One of the professors offered Mr. Bullock One Million Dollars for one of the petrified eggs and the rights to claim it as his own discovery.

Mr. Bullock refused, those men that laughed at him couldn't pay him enough to give them credit for his discovery.

The strength of character and attitudes reflected in these true life stories are reflected in this novel. It is my hope that this novel provides to those of us that are descendants of this great man a little insight as to who he was, what he cared about and some knowledge he wanted to pass on. Marvin C Crowther. Grandson of the author